"I could offer to buy out your contract?"

Emma made her eyes widen even though inside she was burning with rage. Did he think his money could buy him whatever he wanted? "Make it worth my while to leave, you mean?"

"Of course. I can be very *generous* if I need to be."

His quiet boast appalled her, but what appalled her even more was her body's instinctive response to the velvet caress of his voice. For a moment her breasts began to prickle in a way that was alien to her and disbelievingly, she acknowledged it as the ache of sexual desire.

She sat back in her chair and fixed him with a steady look—because she'd seen worse things in her time than some bullying tycoon with a mistaken belief that he had the right to vet his brother's friends. "I hate to disappoint you, Mr. Constantinides, but I'm perfectly happy with my job, and as long as I continue to perform it to everyone's satisfaction, then I'd prefer to carry on just as I am if it's all the same with you."

Staring into her pale green eyes, Zak saw the light of determination and recognized that she had a streak of stubbornness that would not be swayed by the force of his will. She was an employee and she was a woman and *she was daring to defy him!*

What His Money Can't Buy

These powerful men have everything—except the perfect wife!

Zac Constantinides and Ciro D'Angelo are among the richest men in the world.

They share a passion for luxury, opulence and beauty.

So it's no wonder these international playboys strike a deal on London's premier hotel, The Granchester!

The only thing each has yet to acquire is a suitable wife....

The polished beauties who usually adorn their arms are fine for the bedroom, but not the home.

One thing is for sure—it will take a special kind of woman to tame these tycoons!

Watch the sparks fly in Sharon Kendrick's *fabulous* new duet:

Playing the Greek's Game

As Zac takes ownership of the hotel, he is shocked to find the Granchester's designer with her red-painted claws already in his brother! Emma is furious at her new boss's insinuations and just can't wait to take him down a peg or three!

A Tainted Beauty

As Ciro passes from the Granchester to his next acquisition, he's caught off guard by Lily's innocent beauty and is determined to have her as his wife. It's inconceivable that he could have gotten her so wrong, but now that he's married there'll be no turning back.

Sharon Kendrick

PLAYING THE GREEK'S GAME

HARLEQUIN®

entertain, enrich, inspire™

Recycling programs
for this product may
not exist in your area.

ISBN-13: 978-0-373-13088-7

PLAYING THE GREEK'S GAME

Copyright © 2012 by Sharon Kendrick

www.Harlequin.com

Printed in U.S.A.

All about the author…
Sharon Kendrick

SHARON KENDRICK started storytelling at the age of eleven and has never really stopped. She likes to write fast-paced, feel-good romances with heroes who are so sexy they'll make your toes curl!

Born in west London, she now lives in the beautiful city of Winchester—where she can see the cathedral from her window (but only if she stands on tiptoe). She has two children, Celia and Patrick, and her passions include music, books, cooking and eating—and drifting off into wonderful daydreams while she works out new plots!

Visit Sharon at www.sharonkendrick.com.

Other titles by Sharon Kendrick available in eBook:

Harlequin Presents®

To Diana Vinoly, for her invaluable help with interior design—and for letting me into some of her New York secrets!

And for the charity
CHILDREN with CANCER UK,
which does such amazing work.

CHAPTER ONE

EMMA's heart thundered as she stepped into the minimalist penthouse office, but the man sitting at the desk didn't even bother to lift his dark head.

Light streamed in from the enormous windows which overlooked one of London's loveliest parks. It was a view for which the world-renowned Granchester was famous—and which helped make the prices of the landmark hotel so eye-wateringly high. But the magnificence of the view paled in comparison with the formidable man who sat working, his attention fixed on the pile of papers before him.

Zak Constantinides.

The watery November sunshine highlighted the coal-black tumble of his hair and emphasised the musculature of his body. His broad shoulders were hunched and tense. Raw masculinity seemed to pulsate from his powerful frame and the thunder of Emma's heart now became an unsteady beat as she stared at him.

She was nervous. More nervous than she'd been in a long while—and maybe that wasn't surprising. Her boss was making an unscheduled London appearance and she'd been summoned up to see him in his private lair, with no warning whatsoever. And someone as powerful as the Greek tycoon didn't normally bother with people like her.

She'd been halfway up a ladder when the summons had come—and it showed. Beneath her faded jeans and loose T-shirt she was hot and sticky—and strands of hair were falling out of her ponytail. It wasn't exactly the best way to present herself to the powerful billionaire—but there wasn't a lot she could do about it, given that her comb was sitting in her handbag, tucked away in a staff locker somewhere in the bowels of the building.

He must have known she was standing there but he just carried on working as if the room were empty, leaving her feeling as if she were somehow invisible. Unless that was a deliberate ploy on his part. A way of showing her just who was in the driving seat. As if he *needed* to—when the sense of influence and privilege in the air was so heavy you could almost reach out and touch it. But hadn't his brother told her that Zak was a total control freak who enjoyed the weight of his own power?

Feeling like a rookie politician about to make her maiden speech, she cleared her throat. 'Mr Constantinides?'

At this, he lifted his ebony head to reveal hard, rugged features and gleaming olive skin. So far, so Greek. But Zak Constantinides broke the mould with eyes which were grey, instead of the more predictable brown. They surprised her and everyone else who saw them because they were as unsettling as a stormy sky.

They flicked over her now and captured her in their strange, pewter light.

And something inside her tightened. Something she didn't recognise but which filled her with a certain feeling of foreboding. Probably just nerves. Because what else could it be? She didn't *do* men and she certainly didn't do control-freak billionaires who were rumoured to have harem amounts of women dotted around the globe.

His eyes narrowed. *'Ne? Ti thelis?'*

Emma tried an uncertain smile. Had he spoken in his native tongue to distance himself even further, when she knew that his English was as fluent as hers? If so, it had worked, because now the palms of her hands were growing clammy. 'I'm Emma Geary. I believe you wanted to see me?'

Zak leaned back in his chair, his slow scrutiny never faltering as he drifted his gaze over her. 'Indeed I do,' he said softly as he indicated the chair in front of him. 'Please sit down, Miss Geary.'

'Thank you,' she said, horribly aware of the safety pins which were attached to the front of her T-shirt and a strand of hair which was now clinging to her sticky cheek. Was that why his expression was so unsettling— because she looked scruffy, as anyone *would* look if they'd been standing on a ladder hanging curtains for most of the morning?

As the Granchester hotel's in-house interior designer, she'd been busy working on one of the smaller bedrooms on the seventh floor when she'd received the call from his assistant. 'Get up to the boss's penthouse office immediately,' she'd been told. There had barely been time to draw breath before taking the elevator up here in response to his imperious command—and suddenly she wished she'd had time to put on a little make-up. Or substitute a less casual top. Or something. Something which would mean he wouldn't look at her with those stormy eyes boring into her.

Rather self-consciously, she fixed him with an apologetic look. 'I'm sorry I didn't have time to change—'

'Don't be. This isn't a fashion show,' he drawled, his gaze automatically taking in the way the faded denim clung to her slim legs, and the baggy T-shirt, which couldn't disguise the provocative curve of her breasts. Only her hands looked groomed—and Zak liked his women to look groomed. Her nails were long and neatly painted in a bright coral, which made him think about the spectacular sunsets of his native Greece and the soft lap of the nearby sea. Had she known he was looking at them and was that why her hand suddenly fluttered to her chest, drawing attention to the lush jut of her breasts? Unexpectedly, he felt a kick of lust, followed by the slow simmer of fury, but he kept his face impassive. 'What you wear won't have any effect on what I'm about to say to you.'

'Gosh.' She attempted another smile. 'That sounds ominous.'

'Does it?' came his unhelpful response.

Emma's smile wavered as she slid onto the chair facing him and she could do nothing to prevent the whisper of awareness from creeping over her skin as she met that cool grey gaze. But she felt bewilderment, too—

because she didn't do the instant-attraction thing. Not any more. She was like one of those women who hadn't eaten chocolate in so long that just the thought of it now made her feel sick. And so it was with her and men. Or rather, that was the way it usually was.

Just that right now her normal indifference seemed to have deserted her—leaving her feeling strangely vulnerable in front of the hard-faced man who was staring at her so intently. Maybe it was because she'd never been alone with him before. Or maybe because it seemed strangely *intimate* to find the Greek tycoon working diligently at his desk, casually dressed in shirt-sleeves. Especially here.

Because Zak Constantinides usually stayed away from the London side of his worldwide operations—leaving the day-to-day running of his Granchester hotel to others. Happier in New York City, he was known to the staff of the hotel more by reputation than association.

Apart from one brief conversation, Emma had only ever really seen him in passing—for he was not known for engaging with his staff at a personal level. He left that to Xenon, his aide, and, to a lesser extent, to his younger brother, Nat. The last time she'd crossed paths with him had been at an official function here, at the opening of the refurbished Moonlight Room—an operation which she had overseen and been proud of.

She remembered being introduced to him—when his manner towards her had been decidedly lukewarm. His smile had been perfunctory as he'd thanked her for her creative input and she'd got the distinct impression that he'd simply been going through the motions of being polite. But Emma hadn't cared. She hadn't taken it personally because she knew what people said about him. She knew about his meteoric rise in the world of business, his cold heart and the legions of women who lusted after him.

Zak Constantinides was something of a legend—both in and out of the boardroom. He was the kind of man that any sensible woman would steer clear of if she wanted to avoid trouble. Particularly someone like her—who seemed to attract troublesome men, like a moth to the flame.

A long time ago, Emma had realised that she was useless when it came to the opposite sex—a trait which, sadly, she seemed to have inherited. Just like her mother, she'd made bad choices in the past, and had lived to regret the consequences. These days she kept men at a distance and protected her heart and her body from anyone who seemed as if they might be interested in one or either. It was easier that way.

Trying to deep breathe her way to a feeling of calmness, she studied the man sitting in front of her. On the night of the Moonlight's opening, he'd been wearing a black tux—and the exquisite cut of the formal suit had made him look like the powerful tycoon he was.

But today he looked different.

His rough cream cambric shirt was unbuttoned at the neck and rolled up to his elbows to reveal a pair of hair-roughened forearms. His hands were large and strong and his shoulders broad and powerful. It occurred to her that she'd never seen anyone look so unashamedly *mas-*

culine before. He didn't look remotely like a tycoon—
but as if he'd be more at home toiling the land. Or at
least doing something more *physical* than attending to
the pile of papers which were placed in front of him.

He put his pen down and leaned farther back in the
chair and Emma was suddenly made acutely aware of
the heavy material of the shirt straining across the muscular expanse of his chest.

'Any idea why you're here?' he questioned idly.

She gave a little shrug, telling herself she had nothing to feel nervous about. 'Not really. I've been rack-
ing my brains about it on the way here, but no.' There
was a pause as she met the pewter gleam of his eyes.
'I hope you're not dissatisfied with my work, Mr
Constantinides?'

Zak noted the faint flush which had stained her
cheeks and the pale blond lashes which framed her
green eyes, interested to note that she wasn't wearing
make-up. Wouldn't it be easier if he *was* dissatisfied?
If he could just pay her off with the obligatory inflated
fee and tell her to get the hell out of his brother's life?

He'd inherited her when he had taken over the hotel
two years earlier and had seen no reason to change.
He'd bought the Granchester because it had been his
life's ambition to do so—not because he wanted to alter
what was already a very successful concept. Not for
him the expensive makeover, just for the sake of it.
He'd learnt that fortunes could go just as quickly as
they came—and, although he was generous, he rarely
squandered money. Emma Geary was good at her job
and had done a very successful job decorating the land-

mark hotel—and Zak was too much the consummate businessman to want to sacrifice talent, unless it was absolutely necessary.

Only now it seemed that maybe it was.

Because now it seemed that this woman with the pale hair and the coral nails had got her hooks into his baby brother.

The curious thing was that she wasn't what he'd been expecting. He was aware that he'd met her before but could barely remember doing so. He ran across scores of women every day of the week and this one was most definitely not his type—even if he hadn't been programmed to distrust curvy blondes with long legs and soft lips. The photos of her which had been sent to him by the private investigator had been old photos—of a vibrant and colourful creature who bore little resemblance to the woman who sat in front of him now in her old work-clothes.

She didn't look a bit like his brother's usual type, either. Not with that fragile, English appearance and skin so fine and delicate that it seemed it might bruise if you so much as breathed on her.

Maybe that was what had set the alarm bells ringing…along with reports of Nat's increasingly documented appearances with her. Because hadn't he been worried about how his brother was going to cope with the massive inheritance which was due to come his way any day now? And hadn't his worst fears been confirmed when he'd had his new and serious-sounding girlfriend checked out and discovered what kind of woman Emma Geary really was?

On the top of his polished desk, his hands clenched into fists and then slowly unflexed again, so that his long fingers lay splayed across its shiny surface. 'No, I am not dissatisfied with your work,' he said slowly. 'In fact, your work is excellent.'

'Thank heavens for that!' she replied. Be keen, she told herself. Make sure he knows how enthusiastic you are about his hotel. How much you value being an employee. 'We got a pretty decent write-up in the press for the new bar—I don't know if you saw all the clippings I sent out to your New York office? Oh, and I've got lots of plans for the refurbishment of the Garden Room. Big plans! I thought we could do a tie-in with the Chelsea Flower Show—that would be *very* prestigious. In fact...' But her eager words died on her lips as he held up an imperious hand to silence her.

'I haven't brought you up here to discuss refurbishment, Miss Geary,' he said coolly. 'It's a little more personal than that. You see, I've been speaking to my lawyers about your contract.'

'Your lawyers?' Emma stared at him in confusion, not caring that she sounded like a parrot as she repeated his words. 'My contract?'

He frowned, as if to indicate that he didn't welcome the interruption. 'And they told me something rather interesting. You see, it's highly *unusual* for an interior designer to be contracted exclusively to a hotel, rather than as a self-employed consultant.'

Still slightly concerned as to why he'd been talking to his lawyers about her, Emma guessed he was owed some sort of explanation. 'It is a little unusual,' she conceded. 'But it was your predecessor who gave me the permanent contract.'

Zak frowned. 'You mean Ciro D'Angelo?'

'Yes.' Emma remembered the handsome, thirty-something Italian hotelier who'd been so kind to her when she was at her lowest ebb. When she had arrived in London feeling as if her world had reached rock-bottom and Ciro D'Angelo had stepped in and offered her what had seemed like a heaven-sent opportunity. And she had seized the unexpected security he had offered her, like the lifeline it had been. 'Ciro really liked my work. Liked it enough to make me an in-house designer for the Granchester. He said it would give me security. He's a very…a very kind man.'

'He is also,' said Zak repressively, because 'kind' was not a word he had ever heard associated with the ruthless Neapolitan businessman who dated some of the world's most beautiful women, 'a very attractive and exceedingly *rich* man—as well as being an international playboy.'

Tempted to say, *And so are you!* Emma blinked at him in confusion. 'I'm sorry. Am I missing something? I don't see what Ciro's status has to do with anything.'

'Don't you?' Zak gazed at the tremble of her lips and wondered if that glimpse of very feminine fragility was contrived. Was it supposed to make him melt, as other men had undoubtedly melted? In which case, wouldn't it be best that she realised it was completely wasted on him—and that maybe he should start being straight with her? 'Then perhaps I ought to enlighten you. You see, I've been doing a little bit of research on you, Miss Geary.' He paused, and when he spoke again his voice had grown steely. 'And it seems that you have something of a reputation as a femme fatale.'

Emma stared at him, a whisper of fear beginning to shimmer over her skin as long-suppressed echoes of the past began to stir. 'I don't…I don't know what you're talking about.'

'Really?' He heard the lie in her voice and a steely determination entered his body as he noted that all the blood had drained from her face, leaving it almost translucent in its whiteness. He could see the fine blue tracery of veins at her temple and, for some bizarre reason, he found himself wondering whether the skin on the rest of her body was as delicate.

Furious with himself for his wayward thoughts, he hardened his voice. 'You just *happen* to persuade one of the world's sharpest businessmen to give you a permanent contract in his hotel? A lot of people might wonder why that had happened and then leap to the very obvious solution.'

Emma flinched at the insinuation. 'Then a lot of people wouldn't know what they were talking about!'

'They say there's no smoke without fire.'

'"They" say a lot of things, Mr Constantinides—but that doesn't necessarily mean they're the right things.'

'But now Ciro D'Angelo is off the scene. He sold me this hotel and has gone back to live in Naples,' he continued, leaning forward by a fraction because he wanted to see just how she would react to his next charge. 'And since then, you have grown increasingly close to my younger brother.'

Emma felt her body stiffen as the distance between them diminished and she caught a faint but intoxicating drift of sandalwood. Was he aware of the impact which his powerful proximity could have on people? she wondered. And did he use it like a weapon in order to intimidate them, as he was intimidating her now? She suspected he did. 'You mean Nathanael?'

'I have only one brother, Miss Geary.'

Her heart was beating very fast, but she was determined not to crumble. What had Nat told her? That his older brother was used to getting whatever he wanted, whenever he wanted. *And he didn't care who he had to squash in order to accomplish that.* 'And what if I have? Surely getting close to someone isn't a crime?'

'Not a crime, no,' he agreed evenly. 'Although when a woman who makes it her business to cultivate relationships with rich men, starts hitting on Nat—it doesn't exactly fill me with joy.'

She looked at him steadily. 'I don't intend to rise to your insulting inference that I'm some kind of gold-digger. Surely your lawyers didn't advise you to take *that* line of questioning, Mr Constantinides?'

Her cool defiance made his hackles rise and he tightened his knuckles against the shiny surface of the desk. Had Nathanael been foolish enough to blurt out just how much money he was due to inherit? And wouldn't a woman with a track record like hers have seen the green light beckoning and rushed straight in?

Zak felt his mouth tense, felt the painful thunder of his heart as he thought about the little brother he had protected all his life. Whom he had done his best to shield from the harsher aspects of existence after the heartbreaking start he'd had. Only now he was discovering that it was impossible to protect someone completely unless you locked them in a room and threw away the key…and nobody could ever do that to Nat.

'You're wasting your time, Miss Geary.'

'Wasting my time?' she repeated blankly.

'That's right.' His voice lowered and he could feel the breath thicken in his throat, could feel it pushing the words out as if they were dry stones. 'You see, it doesn't matter how wide you open those big green eyes or shake your pale hair—Nathanael isn't in the market for any kind of serious relationship.'

If his whole demeanour hadn't been so deadly serious, Emma might have laughed at just how wrong he had got it. Yes, she'd grown close to Nat and, yes, she counted him as one of her dearest friends. Since his older brother had taken over the Granchester, they'd hit it off like peaches and cream and had always been there for each other. True, he *had* once made a pass at her—but she suspected that had been more out of habit than desire. Almost as if he'd thought it was expected of him. And once she'd batted him away and told him that she wasn't interested—just as she'd once told Ciro she wasn't interested—they had gone on to forge a friendship which was relaxed simply *because* there was no sexual tension.

Emma had found comfort and solace in their innocent companionship. So what right did this tyrant brother have to tell her to lay off?

She found herself wishing she'd been able to speak

to Nat before she'd come up here—but he'd been in a meeting. And suddenly Emma found herself wondering whether her urgent summons had been timed to coincide with Nat's temporary absence.

'And is Nat aware of what you're saying to me?' she questioned slowly. 'Does he know that you're making decisions on his behalf? Because although he works for the family business—I really think he should be the one to decide on his fate and the people with whom he associates, not you.'

'He is not in the market for any kind of relationship,' he repeated as if she hadn't spoken—although the spark of fire in her eyes made him realise that she would not easily be deterred. And that maybe it was time to let her know the truth. Or rather that *he* knew the truth. And perhaps then she would start seeing things his way, the way that people inevitably did. 'But especially not with a woman like you.'

Emma stilled, all her bravado crumbling as the fear she'd suppressed now started rising. Rising and rising and skittering over her skin. Making her feel all dark and icy as she read something dangerous in the depths of his steely eyes. And something told her that she had been rumbled. That you could try to run from the past but you could never completely escape from it. 'A woman like me?' she whispered.

He saw her guilt and a vice-like clamp of triumph gripped him. 'I wonder why you don't work under your married name. Is there a reason for that? A reason why you seem to have airbrushed your past from your CV?' he questioned, looking down at one of the sheets of paper before him. 'Because isn't your real name Emma Patterson—and weren't you once the wife of the rockstar Louis Patterson?'

Emma felt the blood drain from her face and the fingers which had been loosely clasped in her lap now dug painfully together. Yes, it was the past all right—come back to haunt her just as she'd always feared it would. Had she been naive to suppose that she could lose herself in the present—like everyone said you were supposed to—when the dark tentacles of an earlier life were always waiting to pull you back?

'Aren't you?' he persisted.

She swallowed. 'Yes,' she said quietly. 'Yes, I am.'

He lifted his gaze—only now it was cold and condemnatory as it sliced through her like a pewter sword. 'Your ex-husband died through drug abuse,' he said harshly. 'So tell me this, Mrs Patterson. Are you a junkie, too?'

CHAPTER TWO

THE words of Zak Constantinides hit Emma like a hail of bullets. Words she thought she'd left behind a long time ago. Words like *junkie* and *abuse*—and all the terrible associated memories which came with them.

Fighting against a rising tide of nausea, she stared at her boss as the Greek angrily repeated his charge against her.

'Do you take drugs, Miss Geary?'

'No—*no*! I've never touched them—never! You've got no right to accuse me of something like that!'

'Oh, but that's where you're wrong. I've got every right to protect my brother from women with dodgy pasts!'

With an effort, Emma sucked in a deep breath in an attempt to control her ragged breathing but she could do nothing about the wild acceleration of her heart. 'I was married to a man who abused drugs and alcohol, Mr Constantinides,' she said in a low voice. 'I had no idea of that when we met. I was very young and I made a mistake. Have you never made a mistake?'

Grimly, Zak shook his head. Not with relationships

he hadn't, no—he made sure of that. And the occasional slip-up in business had been far too minor to ever qualify as a true mistake. But this was different. Very different. He was known for his old-fashioned and traditional values and he was proud of them. And a woman who had lived the life that Emma Geary had lived would certainly never be welcomed into the arms of *his* family.

He began to pull a series of photos from an envelope on his desk and Emma's face blanched as she fixed her eyes on them. They were old photos. *Very* old photos—but she recognised them instantly.

'Recognise these?' drawled Zak Constantinides.

She forced herself to look at the image which was on top of the gleaming pile he had spread over the desk, like a croupier fanning out a pack of cards. It was of her and Louis on their wedding day.

The press had gone mad—but then, it had been a big story at the time. A nineteen-year-old nobody marrying a rock-star more than twice her age. Emma flinched as she looked at her face in the photo, marvelling at how young she'd been. She'd worn a garland of wildflowers in her hair and a floaty dress of silk chiffon. Her blond hair had hung almost to her waist and the overall effect had been that of some kind of flower fairy who had wandered into the city by mistake. Or at least, that was what Louis had said. He'd even written a song about it on their honeymoon, between slugs of the bourbon bottle, which was never far from his side.

'Of course I recognise it,' she said flatly, her fingers straying to the other pictures—forcing herself to confront them as if to demonstrate to Zak Constantinides that she wasn't afraid.

But she was afraid. She was afraid of the pain which the past could still provoke. She studied the familiar images of her and Louis leaving restaurants—with her supporting her husband and trying desperately not to let the waiting press see his lurching stagger. Some of the shots were of the interiors of once-iconic nightclubs, which had long since disappeared. The blonde girl in the thigh-skimming dress dancing wildly on the podium now seemed like a stranger to her. She had tried so hard to please Louis. To be what he'd wanted her to be. It was what her mother told her that men desired. It was only afterwards, at the sordid end to the marriage, that Emma realised that her mother was the worst possible role model she could have adopted.

'You must have gone to a lot of trouble to get these,' she said, praying that her voice wouldn't betray her with a tremble. 'It's nearly ten years ago.'

'Ten years is nothing—and information is always easy to find if you look in the right places.' Slightly appalled at his own sudden jerk of lust, he pushed one of the photos out of sight—the one which showed the disturbingly distracting image of her shaking her bead-covered bottom in time to the music. He swallowed. 'But you must admit that you aren't my number-one choice as prospective sister-in-law.'

She saw the sudden tightening of his features and knew that she could not let him browbeat her like this. 'Do you always assume that marriage is on the cards whenever your brother dates? Isn't that what's known as jumping the gun?'

'I base my assumptions on experience,' he responded acidly. 'And I know women well enough to understand the lure of vast amounts of money. The Constantinides name is usually enough to guarantee instant devotion from the opposite sex.'

'Even in your case?' she flared.

'Even in mine,' he conceded.

She heard the sarcasm in his voice and was just about to leap to her own defence. To tell him that he'd got it completely wrong and that she and his brother were nothing more than good friends. But something stopped her and she recognised it as the desire to want to hurt him back. To attack him as he had just attacked her by delving into her painful past. It bothered him to think she was in a relationship with his brother, did it? Well, *good*! Let it bother him a bit more until she had the chance to speak to Nat herself.

'It's very difficult for me to tell you exactly what I think of your outrageous accusations since you happen to be my employer,' she said quietly. 'And you seem draconian enough to try to fire me if I speak my mind.'

'On the contrary.' He scowled. 'Your English employment laws seem designed to protect the employee instead of the boss and therefore I can't give myself the satisfaction of firing you unless you do something so outrageous that you really give me no choice.'

Briefly, she wondered whether hurling the pottery jar of pencils at his smug face would qualify as grounds for dismissal, but she kept her hands planted firmly in her lap.

'Then, unfortunately, you seem stuck with me,' she responded and saw his face darken in response to the studied sweetness in her voice.

'Unfortunately, I do,' he agreed, and leaned back in his chair. 'Unless we could come to some mutually agreeable arrangement?'

'Such as?'

He shrugged. 'I could offer to buy out your contract?'

Emma made her eyes widen even though inside she was burning with rage. Did he think his money could buy him whatever he wanted? 'Make it worth my while to leave, you mean?'

'Of course.' He wondered how much it would take to guarantee her departure and his voice dipped as he now found himself around the familiar territory of the negotiating table. 'I can be very *generous* if I need to be.'

His quiet boast appalled her but what appalled her even more was her body's instinctive response to the velvet caress of his voice. For a moment her breasts began to prickle in a way which was alien to her and, disbelievingly, she acknowledged it as the ache of sexual desire.

Self-recrimination flooded through her and Emma prayed that it would dull the hot, melting tightness in her stomach. How could she possibly find him sexy—him of all people? She didn't find *any* men attractive—and especially not the kind of men who thought so little of women in general and her in particular that he thought he could just buy her out, like some sort of commodity.

For a moment she was tempted to play along with him. To name a sum outrageous enough to shock him and then to tell him that she had been testing him. But instinct told her to proceed carefully. Already, Zak Constantinides didn't like or approve of her and, while she wasn't looking for either of those things from him, she'd be unwise to make him an outright enemy, unless she had some sort of industrial death wish.

Instead she sat back in her chair and fixed him with a steady look—because she'd seen off worse things in her time than some bullying tycoon with a mistaken belief that he had the right to vet his brother's friends. 'I hate to disappoint you, Mr Constantinides, but I'm perfectly happy with my job—and as long as I continue to perform it to everyone's satisfaction, then I'd prefer to carry on just as I am, if it's all the same with you.'

Staring into her pale green eyes, Zak saw the light of determination and recognised that she had a streak of stubbornness which would not be swayed by the force of his will. She was an employee and she was a woman and *she was daring to defy him*! And yet his sense of outrage was pacified by the prospect of a looming battle—for he liked nothing more than a fight.

Because he liked to win. He enjoyed the sweet taste of victory. Wasn't that what drove his ambition—what fired up his constant need to acquire new businesses? For a man in his position, there was little that could not be had for the asking—or the taking—yet it seemed that Miss Emma Geary was determined to hang on to her job, even though he wanted her to go.

For a brief moment he thought of sacking her and daring her to sue him—for he had never known anything but triumph in the courtroom. But Zak had neither the time nor the appetite for a courtroom drama—nor any of the attendant publicity. Wouldn't it satisfy him more if he could drive her away by making her realise that it was pointless trying to oppose him?

'I can see that you are a very obstinate woman, Miss Geary,' he said slowly.

'Obstinacy is probably something you're well qualified to recognise, Mr Constantinides.'

He nodded, as if conceding the point. 'You might be interested to know a little more about the chat I had with my lawyers.'

Emma stared at him suspiciously. 'Should I be?'

'I think you should. Because they informed me that there's nothing in your contract which stipulates that you must work in my London hotel.'

It was the expression on his face as much as the sudden change in tone which warned Emma that there was trouble ahead. The granite-hard line of his lips suddenly became the smug little curve of a smile. She fixed him with a questioning look, determined not to show any weakness even though inside her heart was now pounding with fear.

'But I've always worked here,' she objected, her voice rising on a protest. 'At the Granchester.'

'I know you have—and that's why I thought it might be considerate to offer you the chance to work at one of my other hotels. As you know, the Constantinides brand is represented on every continent. Wouldn't it be fun to go abroad?' He raised his eyebrows at her in arrogant question. 'And I'm sure it would do your design career nothing but good to get a little experience elsewhere.'

Furiously, Emma realised exactly what he was doing. He was going to offer her a job as interior designer in one of his Caribbean hotels—or maybe one of the smart city ones. It would be the kind of job which most people in her profession would bite off his hand to be offered—and she would look a complete fool if she turned it down. But she knew what the truth behind such a supposedly generous offer really was.

'You want to get me away from Nat,' she said dully. 'At any cost.'

'Bravo, Miss Geary,' he answered softly. 'You've got it in one.'

'Does Xenon know what you're proposing?'

'Why, have you got him in your pocket, too?' he accused.

'I'm not going to dignify that remark with an answer, Mr Constantinides.'

'Xenon's in charge of the day-to-day running of this hotel!' he snapped. 'But ultimately I'm the one who decides what happens. If I want changes made—then those changes will be made, without me having to run it past anyone else.'

'And if I refuse?'

'Then I think you *will* find you're in breach of contract. And in that case, I would be perfectly within my rights to ask you to leave.'

He leaned back in his chair, his eyes drawn to the luscious thrust of her breasts, and for one brief moment he found himself wishing that Nat had found himself another girlfriend. Any girlfriend except this one. Because her spirited response had unexpectedly ignited his sexual appetite and he could feel its ache deep in his groin. Nobody was usually so spectacularly rude to him—nobody else would have dared to be. And if his brother weren't involved—mightn't he be tempted to ask her to go home and get ready to have dinner with him? To put on a pretty dress that skimmed her delicious bottom and to leave the pale tumble of her blond hair free enough for him to run his fingers through it? Because didn't spirited women make the very best lovers, even if they weren't the best choice of wife?

He looked at her face to see that her eyes were now glaring at him and something in their pistachio fire made his blood grow heated. 'You have some objection perhaps?' he questioned idly.

'Why, you're nothing but a great big *bully*!' she breathed.

He shrugged. 'Your insults are redundant. Take it or leave it. The pay-off still stands if you decide on the latter.'

'Oh, no!' she said quietly. 'I don't give in to blackmail. Or threats. I think you'll discover that you can't get rid of me quite so easily, Mr Constantinides.'

'Really? We'll see about that. In the meantime, why don't you give it some thought? That's all,' he added dismissively. 'You can go now.'

Her face scarlet with rage, Emma rose to her feet— tempted once again to hurl the contents of the pencil pot at his infuriating head. But she concentrated on exiting his office with as much dignity as possible.

She had just reached the door when his voice halted her.

'Oh, and Emma?'

It was the first time he'd used her Christian name and to hear it spoken in that gravelly Greek voice sounded so sinfully irresistible that she found herself turning round to look at him, her heart pounding painfully in her chest.

'What?'

Zak's eyes narrowed as he watched her and something about the way she held herself only increased the flicker of lust he'd felt earlier. She really did have the most amazing *posture*, he thought suddenly. Despite the worn and dishevelled clothes, she moved like a catwalk model. As if she were *gliding* across the room, rather than walking. 'You could always look on this as a sort of test. To see whether your commitment to Nathanael survives an enforced absence. Who knows— it could even strengthen the relationship between you.'

For a moment she really thought he meant it. That he actually cared enough about his brother to test a relationship which didn't really exist. Until she saw the cold glitter of his pewter eyes and realised that this was about nothing more than his legendary control. He didn't care what Nat wanted. Or what she wanted. He just cared about Number One. What *he* wanted. All thoughts of dignity forgotten, Emma felt her blood boil as she turned her back on him.

'You can keep your job offer and you can go to hell,'

she retorted, wrenching open the door to meet the eyes of his startled-looking assistant who was sitting in the outer office. 'Except that the devil probably wouldn't let you in on the grounds that he couldn't stand the competition!'

And she slammed the door on his soft and mocking laughter.

CHAPTER THREE

'THE man is a complete and utter *tyrant*!'

'I *did* warn you.'

'Yes, I know you did but...' Emma put her knife and fork down with a clatter and stared into Nathanael's face. It was a face which bore an unmistakable resemblance to his brother—and yet if they had been statues, then the two men would have been carved from very different stone. 'You didn't tell me that he'd be so...so...'

'So what, Em?'

Emma bit her lip as she stared down at the plate of mozzarella salad, which she'd barely touched because her normally healthy appetite seemed to have deserted her. There was nothing between her and Nat other than friendship, and yet she recognised that it wouldn't be the most diplomatic thing in the world to tell him that she'd found his brother sexually intimidating. Actually, she suspected that the seesawing of her emotions had been as much about attraction as intimidation, but that was something she had no wish to examine.

'So determined to get his own way!' she said instead.

'That is generally what tyrants tend to do,' offered Nat drily.

Emma shook her head. For all her outward anger, she had been deeply unsettled by her encounter with Zak Constantinides. He had made her feel stuff she wasn't used to feeling and that had been bad enough. But even worse was the fact that he had forced her to look at the past, a place which she'd hoped she'd left behind for ever.

And the trouble with looking back was that it made you start to pick away at the present—and to wonder if this was the way your life was meant to be. Since their meeting she'd felt...*unsettled.* As if the odd, quiet calm before a storm had suddenly descended on her. 'You'll never believe what he suggested.'

'What?'

She stared into Nat's more traditional inky-black eyes. 'Only that I go and work in one of his other hotels!'

'Which hotel?'

'He didn't say, but what he meant was any hotel that isn't the Granchester—preferably somewhere in a different country. Anything to get me as far away from you as possible—because, apparently, I've got my gold-digging hooks into you.'

'He can't look at a woman without seeing dollar signs in her eyes,' commented Nat wryly. 'Though, to be fair, he's seen enough examples of that particular breed in his time. What did you tell him?'

Expelling a slow breath, Emma sat back in her seat and looked around. She loved this little Italian restaurant. It wasn't far from the Granchester and was just about affordable as long as you stuck to one course, which she insisted was all they needed—as well as always splitting the bill fifty-fifty, much to Nat's amusement.

They often ate here, depending on the current state of Nat's love life. If it was full-on passion, then their meetings tended to be erratic—but if he'd discovered that his latest goddess had feet of clay, then they became more frequent. Nat hadn't been 'in love' for quite some time—and so they'd seen quite a lot of each other. It was easy and it was comfortable and up until this afternoon's meeting with Zak she had been more than happy with the arrangement. But now? Now she felt as if she had been woken from a bad dream and couldn't quite remember what had frightened her so much.

'I told him he could keep his job,' she said, in reply to his question. 'And I told him to go to hell.'

There was a pause while Nat looked at her with an expression on his face she'd never seen before. 'You told *Zak* to go to hell?'

'Actually, I implied that hell was too good for him.'

Nat started laughing. 'I wish I could have seen his face.'

Emma took a quick sip of wine, because thinking about Zak's face wasn't remotely good for her blood pressure.

'Well, I hope I never see him again,' she said quietly, even though her heart leapt at the memory of those intense pewter eyes and hard lips. 'He can keep his job and his outrageous attempts at manipulation. Who the hell does he think he is that he can move people around as if they're pieces on a chequerboard? I'll hand my notice in and go freelance again. There's loads of work in London at the moment.'

Nat frowned. 'But you don't know where the job is, do you? Think about it. It could be great, Em. New York, maybe—you know that Zak has an amazing hotel on Madison, near Central Park? Or in Paris, maybe—he owns a sumptuous place on Av Georges V, right down from the Seine.'

'I know all about your brother's impressive property portfolio, Nat—and I'm not remotely tempted.'

There was a pause. 'Not even as a favour to me?'

'A favour to you?' Putting her glass back down on the table, Emma narrowed her eyes. 'How does that work?'

He shrugged. 'Think about it. Zak's a control freak who likes to keep an obsessive brotherly eye on me.'

'I know. Why *is* that?'

'Because he's terrified that some scheming beauty is going to get her hands on the Constantinides fortune and bleed it dry. It's happened before. My theory is that he hates women. Actually, scrub that—he *does* hate women.' He saw the question in her eyes and gave a grimace. 'It's a long story.'

'I'm not interested in Zak's story,' she said quickly because she didn't want to 'understand' the man. What was there to understand, other than that he was a tyrant? 'It can't be that different from yours, surely?'

'Oh, I think it was worse. He was older, you see— and he bore the brunt of my parents' divorce.' Nat shrugged. 'And he thinks the women I meet are only after me because of my wallet. Not realising that my abundant charm and prowess in bed are what keep them flocking into my arms! He thinks that one day I should go back home and marry a suitable and beautiful Greek woman.'

'And what do *you* think, Nat? Is that what you want? Or aren't you allowed an opinion?'

'Actually, I haven't ruled anything out,' said Nat unexpectedly. 'All I want is the freedom to live my life as I see fit until the time comes when I want to settle down. And that's where you come in, Em. Or, rather, where you could come in.'

'You're not making any sense.'

He leaned across the table and, with his finger, drew a circle on top of her hand. 'If Zak thinks we're in a serious relationship and he's managed to separate us—then, for once, he won't bother checking up on me, will he? He'll think I'm pining for you and he'll want to placate me. Why, he might even actively push other women in my direction to help me forget you! For once I can date women without feeling as if a dragon is breathing over my shoulder. I'll get the freedom I desire—'

'And what will I get, Nat?' she put in quietly. 'Huh?'

He shrugged, his smile gentle. 'The chance to spread your wings? To put something new and wonderful on your portfolio? Why *not*, Em? What's stopping you?'

Emma paused to consider his question. What *was* stopping her? Anger that his billionaire brother could be so outrageously manipulative? Or was it something more fundamental than that…a deep-rooted fear of change itself?

Yet surely no one could blame her for wanting a little stability for the first time in her life. She opened her lips, about to reject his suggestion outright—but something in Nat's words had struck an uncomfortable chord. And once she started thinking about it, she couldn't stop.

The Granchester had provided a place of refuge when she'd most needed it. It had helped her recover from her disastrous marriage and to hone her interior-designing skills. She'd forged a quiet and uneventful life for herself, which had been something she'd always wanted—but hadn't it all become a little too easy?

She knew that her craving for peace had come as a reaction to the past—to avoid repeating those highs and lows she'd found so exhausting. But now she could see that maybe she had allowed herself to fall into a rut and that maybe it was time to clamber out of it. Wouldn't it be good for her to grab this amazing opportunity, even if it had arrived by rather unconventional and unwanted means?

What was the worst thing that could happen? That the arrogant Zak would see her agreement as confirmation that he'd won this little battle? Would that really be so bad? Why not let him have his pathetic few moments of gloating triumph—after all, he was nothing to her.

And the best thing that could happen? Emma stared down at Nat's olive finger which was still drawing little circles over her hand. She'd get a little more breadth on her CV—the extra dimension she needed. Because she was good at her job, she knew she was—and mightn't this be the little push she needed to fulfil her true potential?

'Maybe I'll ring Zak up and tell him I'll take it after all,' she said uncertainly.

'No need to do that,' said Nat, in an odd sort of voice. 'You can tell him yourself, right now.'

Emma stiffened, her horrified gaze travelling to the door to see Zak Constantinides walking into the restaurant as if he owned it. Come to think of it, he probably did. Other heads had also turned to watch him and Emma suddenly realised that he must always have that effect on people. The sense that someone *special* had just walked in. The noise of the room had diminished and a pin-drop silence ensued, before the roar of chatter resumed to a great crescendo.

Her heart began crashing out a crazy rhythm as she registered his powerful frame, kitted out in a dark suit of such impeccable cut that it made every other man in the place look bland. And then she noticed that he wasn't alone. That he had a woman with him. She gave a wry smile. Of course he did. A man like him would have his pick of any number of dates.

The woman looked Greek and was model-slim, her short hair framing sharp cheekbones and elfin features. Few women would have looked so beautiful with such an unforgiving haircut, but this one did. In fact, she looked absolutely stunning. With her retro sixties mini and white over-the-knee boots, Zak's companion looked as if she'd fallen straight from the pages of *Vogue*.

Telling herself to look away but finding it impossible to do so, Emma felt her breath catch in her throat as Zak put a protective hand in the small of the woman's back. She watched as they followed the maître d' to a secluded table in the corner and the woman was just sitting down when Zak glanced up and saw her, his pewter eyes boring into her with a look of disbelief and something else, too. Something she'd never seen in a man's eyes before and which she couldn't even begin to interpret.

Her fingers began trembling and her heart renewed its painful crash against her ribs. Just what was it about him which made her have such a *physical* reaction to him? Which made her mind dance with such disturbing images?

Forcing herself to look away, she glanced down at her untouched plate. 'Did you know he was coming here?' she hissed.

'Of course I didn't!'

'Can't we get the bill and leave?'

'Too late,' said Nat. 'He's coming over.'

To Emma it felt as if she were waiting for her own execution. She could feel her cheeks burning and that strange tingling in her breasts again. And maybe sitting still was her only option because her legs suddenly felt as if they were made of jelly and she didn't think she could have moved anywhere.

He reached them at last, his substantial shadow falling over the crisp white tablecloth like a dark omen and she had no option but to look up from the blur of food still on her plate and into the rugged beauty of his face.

'Well, well, well—if it isn't Miss Emma Geary,' he said softly. 'Dining with my brother. And looking like love's young dream.'

What was it which made Emma curve her lips into a knowing smile and place her hand directly over Nat's in a gesture which spoke of pure possession? Did it have something to do with the cynicism which glittered from Zak's eyes—or was she just trying to shield herself against his undoubted charisma?

'We can't help how we look, can we, Nat?' she questioned softly, and saw the briefest look of surprise in her date's eyes before he shook his head.

'We certainly can't, Em,' he purred obediently.

Looking down at their entwined fingers, Zak flinched at the contrast between Nat's deep olive skin and the pale translucence of hers. Some primeval hostility began to heat his blood—and reasons other than brotherly regard made him wish that he could ship his brother straight back to Greece and into the arms of a woman with a past less chequered than this one.

He turned his attention to his brother. 'Why don't you go over and say hello to Leda?' he questioned, glancing across at the waiting brunette and giving her an affectionate smile. 'You remember her, don't you?'

'I should do—you went out with her for long enough—though I'd never have recognised her with her hair all cut off like that. She looks amazing.' Nat smiled at the woman across the restaurant as he rose to his feet. 'You know, everyone thought you two would get married, Zak.'

Zak didn't answer that, just waited until his brother had reached his dinner date before turning to look down at Emma, and his heart gave an unsteady beat as he did so. Wasn't it strange what a shower and a hair wash and a little make-up could do? Because suddenly her status as a femme fatale became a whole lot more believable than it had been this afternoon. The ponytailed, flustered woman in faded jeans who'd walked into his office was now nothing but a distant memory—banished by the undeniably chic image she presented tonight.

Her dress was simple—a linen shift of pale dove-grey colour—and it was very slightly creased. But the creases didn't matter because the natural fabric showcased her pure, pale skin and the musculature of her fit young body. And Zak realised that anything she wore would simply be a backdrop for that magnificent blond hair—which tonight fell in a moon-pale tumble over her shoulders. It wasn't as long as it had been in that rather hippy-looking wedding photo—but it still waved silkily over her breasts and reminded him of their lush pertness.

To his fury, he experienced a fierce kick of some emotion—a potent mix of jealousy and lust which manifested itself in an urgent desire to drag her to her feet and to kiss her. To crush those petal-soft lips beneath his own. To thrust his tongue deep inside her mouth, and then…

Appalled and very turned on, he swallowed down the acrid taste in his mouth and silently banished his wayward thoughts. Surely he wasn't jealous of his little brother? Or so sexually frustrated that he'd start to desire a woman who couldn't *be* more unsuitable—and on so many levels?

He looked directly at her. 'Have you thought any more about my job offer?'

'I have.'

'And?'

Emma's thoughts whirled as the moment of truth loomed. It was all very well Nat telling her that she should take the job but there was one very good reason why she shouldn't, and he was standing right in front of her. She didn't know what it was about Zak Constantinides which made her react so...so *violently* towards him, but some bone-deep instinct told her to heed it. Yet alongside her misgivings came a powerful urge to teach this arch manipulator a lesson. Wouldn't it be wonderful if she could play the part that Nat wanted her to play and give her dear friend some much-wanted freedom? Wouldn't it give her immense satisfaction to trick this arrogant billionaire and make a mockery of his manoeuvring?

She curved her lips into what she hoped was a suitable smile. 'And I'll accept.'

He frowned. 'Just like that?'

'Just like that. On one condition.'

'Oh, no.' He shook his head. 'I'm the one who lays down conditions, Miss Geary, not you.'

She carried on as if he hadn't spoken. 'That I'm back in London in time for Christmas.'

He had been expecting a demand for some over-inflated bonus and her request took him slightly by surprise. Would almost two months be long enough to have the desired effect? He glanced over to where Nat was chatting animatedly to his date and Zak's lips curved into a smile. Of course it would! His brother would soon forget about Emma Geary. What was it they said? Out of sight, out of mind…

'I don't think that will be a problem,' he said, glancing down at her barely touched plate of food. 'Enjoy your last supper before you take up your assignment.'

'Well, hopefully I'll have time for a few more suppers before I leave.'

'I'd like you to come out this weekend.'

'You're joking?'

His grey eyes bored into her. 'No, Emma, I'm deadly serious.'

It was the way he said her name which made her words stumble. As if it were a big dollop of honey he was slowly licking from a spoon. 'What's the r-rush?'

Enjoying the familiar rush of power and the sudden tremble of her lips, he shrugged. 'Why delay? Protracted farewells are so painful. Far better to make a clean break of it and get used to living without Nat.'

'Where have you got planned for me—Outer Mongolia, I suppose?'

'The Constantinides brand hasn't reached quite that far, but give me time,' answered Zak smoothly. 'No, I'm sending you somewhere far more cosmopolitan than that.'

'And am I allowed to know where—or is it a magical mystery tour?'

He felt a muscle begin to beat at his temple. It was anger but it was something else too—because her insubordination was turning him on. When you reached the position that he'd reached a long time ago, you never got a member of staff speaking to you with quite the same degree of insolence as Miss Emma Geary did to him. Nor anyone else, for that matter. And it was making him want to subdue her in the most fundamental way possible...

'How does New York sound?' he questioned silkily.

For a moment, Emma stilled. Was he some sort of sadist, as well as being a control freak? Didn't he realise that New York was the city she'd lived in during her ill-fated marriage and it was packed full of bad memories? Meeting the obdurate set of his rugged features, she bit back the protest which had sprung to her lips. Because if she showed any weakness, then wouldn't he leap on it like the bully he was?

She set her face into the most vacuous expression she could manage. 'New York?' she questioned, forcing a delight into her voice—a delight she was far from feeling. 'How wonderful! The city that never sleeps!'

He winced at the cliché. 'So they say. I've booked you a ticket for Saturday. A car will pick you up and take you to the airport—my secretary will be in touch with all the details. See you in the "Big Apple", Emma.'

He had walked away before she could say another word but Emma could hardly chase him across the restaurant, demanding to know what he had meant. Surely he didn't mean that *he was going to be in New York at the same time?*

Was that to keep an eye on her? To make sure she did exactly as he wanted?

She didn't know and, right now, she wasn't in a fit

state to care. All she was aware of was a feeling of
trepidation, which had somehow become all mixed up
with a heart-racing excitement she didn't dare analyse.

CHAPTER FOUR

IT was strange being back. Strange to hear the distinctive drawling accents and to watch people rushing everywhere with that particular sense of purpose which you only ever seemed to find in New York. Leaning back against the soft leather seat of the car, Emma watched the blur of skyscrapers appearing in the distance as the plush limousine headed towards the city.

Zak's car had met her at JFK airport even though she would have been perfectly happy to find herself a yellow taxi. More than happy. It might have made her feel normal to have pulled her luggage through the busy terminal like all the other travellers. It might have reinforced an independence she was far from feeling.

Because the weirdest thing was that this trip seemed horribly similar to the first and only other she'd made to America—and that only increased her anxiety level. Because all those years ago, she'd been at the beck and call of a wealthy man who had called all the shots and *now she was in exactly the same position.* The main difference was that Louis had been weak—something her immaturity had failed to pick up on at the time. And

Zak was the opposite. Zak was strong. Inside she knew that, though she wasn't quite sure how. Just something bone-deep and certain assured her that the Greek tyrant had a core of steel.

What did he really want from her? The promise that she would leave his brother alone—was that all he wanted?

The car began travelling downtown and Emma looked out through the smoky windows at the brightly lit department stores. There was Sacs on Fifth—where Louis had once bought her a costly and rather traditional pearl necklace, then been delighted when she'd wrapped it around her blond hair like a coronet. That was one of the better memories—but there were bleak ones, too, piling in on her now like dark spectres.

The giant billboards and lights of Broadway reminded her of the Yankee Stadium where the Patterson band had been poised to make their big comeback—until it was cancelled at the last minute when a shocked promoter realised that the lead singer was barely able to stand. And there was St Patrick's Cathedral, where she'd crept in to light a candle and to quietly weep for the death of her marriage and soon after that, for the death of her husband.

Shaking her head as if to clear some space, she became aware that Central Park was sliding past and that the car was now purring to a halt outside Zak's Pembroke hotel.

She tried to take in all the beautiful details which she'd only ever seen on promotional literature. The art-deco exterior and the revolving door fashioned from rich, dark wood. The lamps made of wrought-iron and the carefully shaped box trees which added a splash of green to the urban environment. A doorman opened the door and she stepped into the gleaming marble lobby to see an enormous chandelier, its diamond shards glittering light down onto ornate displays of flowers.

In the confusion of a changed time zone and being in a foreign city, she felt a little disorientated. Should she go over to the main desk and ask whether Mr Constantinides had left a message for her? Or...

And then suddenly she was aware of a man towering over her. Of the olive-skinned hand which had reached out to pick up her suitcase as effortlessly as if it had been filled with butterflies rather than a rather large amount of shoes.

'Welcome to New York,' said a sexy and horribly familiar voice and she found herself staring up into the granite features of Zak Constantinides. Was that triumph she could read in his grey eyes? Very probably—since he'd got exactly what he wanted. He'd had her being shipped over to New York as if she were some kind of human parcel!

She wanted to react to him with nothing but cool indifference but somehow that wasn't as easy as it should have been. She felt *daunted* by him, and she felt attracted to him, too, despite her determination not to be. It didn't help that today he looked curiously accessible. He wore a soft cashmere sweater of the same hue as his eyes which hugged his muscular torso, along with jeans which emphasised the powerful thrust of his long legs. Once again she found herself acutely aware of his presence as a man and *she didn't want to be aware of him that way*!

Beneath her own warm jacket—bought specially to withstand the potential cold of the November weather— Emma shivered.

'You're cold?' he questioned.

'A bit,' she said airily, terrified that he'd guess her involuntary shudder had been more about desire than temperature. 'I always find American hotels a bit heavy-handed with the air conditioning. And why on earth are you carrying my suitcase?'

'Why not? You object to a little old-fashioned chivalry, do you?'

There hadn't exactly been a lot of old-fashioned chivalry in Emma's life and for a moment she was a little taken aback. 'You greet all your guests in this way, do you?'

'Not all of them, no. But for you, Emma—I'm prepared to make an exception.' The words came out of his mouth before he realised that he meant them. Zak didn't stop to ask himself why he had been watching the clock until he'd heard from his driver that her flight had touched down safely. Or why he'd felt the leap of his heart and the heat of his groin when he'd known that she was heading towards the city.

Yet wasn't the truth of it that he hadn't been able to stop thinking about her? That she had entered his night-time dreams like some pale and unwanted intruder, with her green eyes and the moon-pale spill of her hair. Hadn't he found himself *wanting her* with an ache which had been intense and unfamiliar?

It was interesting that his fantasies weren't matched by the reality of seeing her again—because she certainly hadn't dressed up. Her face was completely bare of make-up, the stark ponytail was back and the clothes she wore beneath her functional jacket were distinctly unimpressive. Her muted appearance should have been a real anticlimax and yet she possessed an indefinable something which made him want to study the way the light fell on her chiselled cheekbones and the faint golden sprinkling of freckles over her nose. Just how did she do that air of vulnerability so beautifully? he wondered. Had she worked on her technique, just as a tennis player might work on her backhand?

'You must be tired,' he said softly as he became aware of the faint shadows beneath her eyes. 'Come with me and I'll show you where you're staying—and then you can start thinking about dinner.'

His words penetrated Emma's befuddled thoughts, shook her out of the somewhat dazed acknowledgement that his gaze was focused on her like a laser beam and that her body was glowing in response. 'You mean, I'm going to be staying *here*? At the Pembroke?'

'Of course you are. As you're only here on secondment for a few weeks it makes much more sense. Where else did you think you'd be staying?'

She'd imagined some small studio apartment on the lower side of town. Somewhere where she'd be woken up by the early-morning sounds of street cleaning and kept awake by late-night revelry. The kind of place where it would be tough to find a taxi. Somewhere as far away from Zak as possible.

'It was such a rush to get out here that I didn't stop to think *where* I'd be staying,' she said, her dismissive air not quite ringing true.

'Well, you're here now—so you can relax.'

She was aware of people staring at them as they crossed the lobby and headed for the elevator. Some of those were the staff, obviously—probably wondering why their boss was carrying the suitcase of this rather ordinary-looking guest. But some of the guests were giving them the once-over, too. Younger women wearing conspicuous signs of wealth had openly envious looks on their faces, while their older male partners glanced up briefly from where they were tapping addictively on their computers.

Zak didn't speak until the elevator doors had shut out the rest of the world and he found himself alone with her. She was staring steadfastly at the red arrow which was indicating the floor count as the lift rode upwards and it was an odd sensation to be in the company of a woman who wasn't focusing her attention entirely on him. 'Not the most enthusiastic response I've ever received from a member of staff who's just been told she's staying in one of the world's finest hotels,' he observed wryly.

Realising that she couldn't keep avoiding his eye, she turned to look at him. 'Are you surprised?'

'I am—a little. I thought you'd revel in the opportunity to enjoy some of the Pembroke's legendary hospitality.'

Emma gave a short laugh because, ironically, he couldn't be more wrong if he tried. Money didn't 'do' it for her. Not any more. She'd learnt that the simple things in life meant more than all the glitz and glamour in the world. She'd seen only too well that wealth could bring with it nothing but emptiness and a great dark void. Until she remembered that she was supposed to be a gold-digger of the first order and so she widened her eyes in the most gold-diggery way she could manage.

'I suppose when you put it like *that*.' Deciding that licking her lips would be a little over the top, she injected a longing note into her voice instead. 'Will I be staying in a *very* big suite?' she questioned.

'Not as big as mine,' Zak murmured as the greedy look in her eyes demanded—and got—a predictably mocking response from him. But he hadn't counted on his body's interpretation of this as some kind of basic flirting. So that hot on the heels of his sardonic retort came an inexplicable need to see her blond hair spread all over the pillow of his vast bed. To see those pale green eyes slitted with desire as she welcomed him into her arms.

Silently he cursed himself as the jerk of an erection made his groin grow heavy. What the hell was he *thinking of*? She was everything he despised in the opposite sex and—even if she hadn't been—*she was dating his brother*.

'We're here,' he said abruptly.

They had reached the thirty-second floor and Emma stepped out, noting the general air of luxury which immediately surrounded her—the gleaming hardwood floors on which lay priceless silk rugs. The walls were hung with original art and most of it was very impressive and she found herself wondering what the Pembroke's nightly rate was.

'Is my room on this floor?' she asked.

'It is. It's right here.' He pushed open the door to her suite. 'Make yourself comfortable and I'll come by and pick you up for dinner.'

Emma forced a smile. 'I think I'd rather order from room service, if it's all the same with you.'

'I disagree—that's the worst way of coping with jet lag. You'll fall asleep and be wide awake in the middle of the night,' he demurred with an emphatic shake of his head. 'And besides, there are things we need to discuss.'

'Things?' She stared at him. 'What kind of things?'

He met the startled greenness of her eyes and once again felt the unwanted punch of desire. 'It's no great mystery. You're here to work, Emma—and so far I haven't told you what you'll be doing. We'll eat downstairs in the restaurant and I'll brief you. I'll pick you up in an hour.'

'An hour and a half,' she amended stubbornly.

'Done.'

He turned and walked away, leaving Emma resisting the desire to watch him. Instead, she went into her room and closed the door behind her, her attention immediately caught by the enormous glass windows.

The view was distracting—a jumble of light-spangled skyscrapers, which together formed the instantly recognisable skyline of New York. It was beautiful, she thought—even if it did bring back some uncomfortable memories and even if she was slightly too tired to appreciate it.

She forced herself to unpack, knowing that if she did it now, it would mean she wouldn't awake to an even bigger chore of badly crumpled clothes. She put her shoes in the wardrobe and her underwear in the walnut drawers and went through to the bathroom to shower, feeling all the travel grime being washed away beneath the warm jets. Afterwards, she brushed her wet hair and pulled on an irresistibly fluffy white bathrobe, thinking that she'd just have a cup of coffee to wake herself up before getting dressed.

She clicked on the machine, turned down the air conditioning and then sat down on the huge bed where giant, squashy pillows were jostling for space. What *was* the collective term for pillows? she wondered dreamily. A pile of pillows, or a heap of pillows? Laying her head down on one of them, she heard the hypnotic gurgle of the coffee machine as her eyelashes drifted to an irresistible close.

Odd sounds began to penetrate her dream. She heard the rattle of a trolley, which made her think she was still on the aircraft, and then some sort of muffled thumping. And the next thing she knew was a hand on her arms, pushing against the fluffy towelling robe, and she fluttered open her eyes to see Zak standing over her, his face dark with an odd kind of tension.

For a moment neither of them spoke—their gazes locking and holding as if time and place had been suspended, leaving them shut in their own private universe. Her heart thundering, she stared up at him with a sudden longing—aware of his proximity and the mesmerising tang of sandalwood. Aware too that she was

completely naked beneath the robe and that her breasts
had started to tingle in response to his narrow-eyed
scrutiny.

'What is it?' she mumbled from between dry lips.

Zak watched as a tiny pink tongue flicked out to
moisten her lips. God, she was beautiful, he thought.
Unbelievably beautiful. 'I couldn't wake you,' he accused thickly.

It occurred to her that he could have phoned her—
but she didn't say so because his hand was still on her
arm and, shamefully, she didn't want him to remove it.
Was that because she was still half asleep and therefore
disorientated—or was the real reason that she *liked* him
touching her? That she was enjoying the sensation of
his fingers pressing through the robe and into her skin.

'Well, you've woken me now,' she said, stifling a
yawn.

Reluctantly pulling his hand away, he walked over
to the window. Staring hard at a view he usually took
for granted, he tried to focus on the brilliant gleam of
the skyscrapers' lights instead of the soft accessibility
of her body beneath the voluminous robe. But it was
damned near impossible. All he could think of was the
translucent quality of her skin and the vulnerability
she'd exuded when she'd been asleep. And then she had
woken and those pale green eyes had slitted open at him
in lazy question, just like in his forbidden fantasy—and
he cursed himself for forgetting two vital facts.

She was not his kind of woman!

More important still, she was his *brother's woman*!

There was no way he could deny the powerful sexual

chemistry which had sizzled between them right from the start—and Zak was far too experienced to pretend it hadn't happened. That it wasn't happening how. And didn't that justify what he was doing by bringing her here to New York? If she could put out like this for her lover's *brother*—then wasn't Nat better off without her?

'I'll be waiting downstairs in the restaurant,' he gritted out. 'Be there in fifteen minutes.'

Emma sat up as he walked straight past the bed without another look in her direction but she could feel the sudden disapproval radiating from his powerful body. What was his problem? Was he angry because he'd just been looking at her as if he'd like to eat her?

And wasn't her problem that she'd wanted him to?

Getting off a bed which now felt contaminated, Emma scrambled to find some underwear, guilt washing over her as she clipped on a lacy black bra—acknowledging the heavy aching in her tender breasts. Because wasn't the pitiful truth of it that she had *wanted* Zak Constantinides in a way she'd never wanted anyone else? She bit her lip in horrified remorse. Not even her own husband!

He must have felt the powerful vibes which had shimmered between them—because you'd need to be made of stone to ignore them. He already thought that she was a sexually voracious gold-digger—so wouldn't her behaviour only reinforce his poor opinion of her?

She needed to pull herself together and she needed to grow a little backbone. She wasn't just some puppet which he could manipulate at will. Hadn't she worked hard at the Granchester—hard enough to establish herself as an interior designer who was respected by others in the business? She'd done all that with determination, hard work and very little in the way of formal training. So was she prepared to let all that crumble away, simply because her body was reacting in a way she didn't want towards a man she didn't like?

No, she was not.

And she would start by sending out the subliminal but very clear message that she was not out to entice him.

She had the kind of looks which she could dress up or down—and tonight was definitely a night for fading into the background. She picked out a pair of black velvet trousers and teamed them with a floaty white shirt. Her hair had acquired a slight kink from where she'd slept on it while it was still damp—so she brushed it and then wove it into a loose bun, which sat on the back of her neck. Make-up she deliberately resisted and a dangly pair of shell earrings was her only adornment. After all—wasn't 'casual' the new black?

But the moment she walked into the restaurant she realised that she was woefully underdressed. Or rather, overdressed. She'd never seen so much flesh on show and every other woman in the room was all buffed and honed and highlighted with the sparkle of jewels.

Emma kept her head high as she gave Zak's name to a rather bemused-looking waiter and as he led her towards the Greek's table she was acutely aware of being watched. She'd forgotten what it was like to be judged by your companion. To have people look you up and down and form an opinion about you when they didn't even know you.

Her stomach was in knots as Zak rose to greet her and she saw that his gaze was hooded. She thought she sensed disapproval as he looked at her—and, although she'd chosen her outfit with just that result in mind, there was a very feminine part of her which cringed beneath his critical scrutiny.

'You look like you're just off to a rock festival,' he commented acidly.

She surveyed the pristine elegance of his dark suit. 'And you look like you're about to perform some hostile boardroom bid.'

For a moment his lips almost curved into a smile, until he reminded himself that he was not here to be amused by her. Maybe it was a good thing that she looked as if she was about to start lighting incense, or sit cross-legged on the floor before starting to meditate. He sat back as the waiter handed her a glossy menu. 'How about I order to save time? The steak here is very good.'

Emma gave a polite smile. 'I'm sure it is, but I don't eat meat.'

'You don't eat meat?'

She raised her eyebrows. 'Which part of my original statement needed clarification, Mr Constantinides?'

He stared at her critically. 'No wonder you're so damned pale.'

'You should try it some time—less meat in the diet is supposed to mean less aggression.'

At this he did laugh. 'A real man eats meat, Emma.'

There was something about his primitive boast which made her feel quite peculiar and Emma quickly looked down at the very limited vegetarian section of the menu.

Did he really think he could come out with all that macho 'real men eat meat' stuff and get away with it? Yes, he did—and the horrifying reality was that he *could*. She suspected he could do pretty well anything he put his mind to, especially where women were concerned. She remembered the way she'd found him looking at her when he'd shaken her awake. That compelling hunger she'd surprised in his eyes. And hadn't that look made her feel a corresponding rush of desire, which had made her feel as if she were melting beneath his gaze?

Suddenly, Emma felt a trickle of fear sliding down her spine because she suspected that Zak Constantinides knew perfectly well the extent of his power over women. And the very last thing she needed was for him to discover that he had awoken a strange and nebulous need in *her*.

'And you're really going to have to lose the "Mr Constantinides" tag,' he mused.

'I would have thought that my constant reinforcement of your superior status would have bolstered your ego.'

'I don't need anything to bolster my ego,' he said softly. 'So do you think you could try saying "Zak"?'

She snapped the menu shut and looked up. 'I'll have the aubergine lasagne and side salad, please.... *Zak*.'

'And I'll have the rib-eye.' He handed the menus to the waiter, thinking that her soft English accent managed to do erotic things with the single syllable of his name. He fixed her with a questioning look. 'Wine?'

She thought she probably shouldn't. In fact, she definitely shouldn't. Wine might make the meal seem like a pleasure, rather than the necessity it clearly was. But Emma was strung out—and the idea of having to endure an evening facing Zak Constantinides without something to help relax her was more than she was prepared to tolerate.

'A glass would be lovely.'

He nodded and the sommelier was dispatched, returning with two glasses of red wine so rich that Emma could smell it from five paces away. She took an eager sip and put the glass down with a little sigh, looking up to meet the curiosity lancing through his grey eyes. 'The wine's very good,' she said politely.

'Of course it's good—do you really think I'd drink anything but the best?'

'Silly of me not to realise that everything you do is a testimony to how wonderful you are.'

'Very silly. But I haven't brought you here to talk about the wine, Emma. Or about me.'

'I didn't think you had,' she said, her heart suddenly beginning to race, because suddenly she suspected what was coming next.

'I want to know what it's like being back in New York,' he questioned—and now his voice took on a harsh tone. 'You lived here when you were married, didn't you?'

So he *hadn't* forgotten that she'd lived here—and he hadn't cared that she might be upset by that fact. Of course he hadn't—for he had made his hostility towards her very clear, right from the start. He didn't care how much she hurt—because he saw her simply as an obstacle to be removed from his brother's life.

She wanted to tell him that her past was none of his business and yet a feeling of resignation made the words die in her throat. Because in a way, hadn't this conversation been inevitable from the moment she'd first walked into his office? He was determined to know more about her and she couldn't *keep* stonewalling questions which were bound to keep coming, could she? It all boiled down to whether she was ashamed of her past. Maybe a *little*—but she was proud of the way she'd risen from the ashes of it to start all over again.

'What is it you want to know?' she questioned.

'I want to know how a small-town English girl managed to meet and marry someone like Louis Patterson. And whether the price you paid for your ten minutes of fame was worth it.'

CHAPTER FIVE

EMMA's fingers tightened around the stem of her wine glass as she met the accusation which glittered from Zak's grey eyes. 'I'm surprised you need to ask me anything about my past—I thought you'd already had me investigated thoroughly by some sleuth you'd hired.'

He took a sip of his own wine. 'I know the facts. What I'm interested in are the reasons behind those facts. And let's face it, Emma—if your relationship with my brother *does* survive this separation...' He paused, not wanting to acknowledge the dark thoughts which flashed into his mind as he tried to envisage this particular scenario. 'If you really *were* to become my sister-in-law—then surely you owe it to me to tell me more about your background.'

'I don't owe *you* anything!'

'No? Then what's the big mystery? Are you ashamed of what you've done? Maybe dabbled in a few things which aren't strictly legal?' he speculated.

'No, I have not!'

'And does Nat know about your past?'

'Of course he does.'

'So why not tell me, too?'

Emma drank down an angry mouthful of wine. Because Nat hadn't judged her as she suspected this man would judge her. Because she didn't fancy being dissected by those cold grey eyes and made to feel like some animal in a laboratory, which was vulnerable to the cruel scalpel of the scientist.

Yet she wasn't supposed to be ashamed of her up-bringing, was she? Not any more. Not when she had coped with it as well as she could. Was it her fault that she'd been given a vacuous and man-hungry mother who had always put her little girl second? Who had taught her daughter all the wrong lessons in life, which had taken a while to unlearn.

'You know I'm illegitimate?' she questioned bluntly.

Her candour took him by surprise and, to his aston-ishment, something in the darkening of her eyes made him want to offer an unlikely chunk of reassurance. 'That's no longer the stigma it was.'

'In *theory* it isn't,' she contradicted. 'In practice it isn't so good if everyone knows that you've never even seen your father—or that you don't have a clue who he is. Or that your mother seeks the comfort of strangers to warm her bed at night.'

Zak's mouth tightened, all sympathy now fled. 'Your mother was a—'

Emma shook her head. 'Oh, she wasn't a prostitute—if that's what you're thinking. She was just very...' she swallowed '...*fond* of men. And not very good at choos-ing men. Something she seems to have passed on to me.'

His eyes narrowed. 'Really?'

'Oh, I'm not talking about Nat,' she amended hastily, remembering a little too late that she was supposed to be masquerading as the lovelorn girlfriend of his brother. 'Nat has been the best thing that ever happened to me.'

'I'm not here to talk about my brother,' he bit back, his blood growing heated with what he suspected was more than a feeling of sibling protectiveness. 'I asked you about Patterson. How did you meet him?'

For a moment Emma said nothing, because it was still painful to relive it. To remember her naivety—a naivety which had been almost laughable in view of the bizarre nature of her upbringing.

'How did I meet Louis?' she repeated. 'Circumstance, I guess.'

'Circumstance?' he echoed.

'That's right. You could never have planned for what happened.'

'Oh?'

There was a moment of silence. 'My mother was a brilliant dancer,' she said at last. 'In another life, she might have done it professionally, but that was almost impossible as a single mother with very little in the way of regular income. Her life was one of constant frustration. Domesticity bored her—she saw it as drudgery—and so did motherhood. So she didn't play board games or read me any bedtime stories, or any of the normal stuff that children get—but she did have a great sense of style, and colour, which I *did* inherit. And, as I say—she was a great dancer.'

Zak nodded as her incredible posture suddenly made

sense. The way she had seemed almost to *float* out of his office. 'She taught you to dance?' he guessed.

'Yes,' said Emma simply, leaning back as the waiter deposited elegant layers of aubergine and pasta before her and trying not to shudder at the sight of Zak's bloody rib-eye steak. 'They were the best times I ever had with her. She'd put the music on really high—sometimes the neighbours would bang on the ceiling with a broom—and we'd wrap ourselves up in floaty shawls, and just dance.'

'And Patterson saw you dancing?' he guessed.

Unwillingly, she gave a nod to his perception. 'Yes, he did. I was exactly eighteen when I met him and had gone to the most fashionable nightclub in London. It was my birthday present from Mum—she'd been saving up for it for ages. She said that every girl on the brink of womanhood should get a glimpse of what the world could offer—that there was glamour out there if only you looked for it. I'd never been anywhere like it before.'

'Never?'

She shook her head. 'It was dark with flashing lights, and the music was thumping out. I didn't really like it. It felt false…*unreal.* There was a big podium at the front—all silver and sparkling—and my favourite song came on. I was feeling a bit out of my depth but that was something familiar. One of my friends egged me on, so I got up and danced my heart out and Louis was sitting in a corner, watching. He said afterwards that—'

'Don't tell me. It was *love at first sight*?' he questioned cynically, imagining the tawdry chat-up lines which must have ensued.

She shrugged. 'That's what he said.'

Hearing the defensiveness in her voice, Zak pushed his plate away. He could imagine just what an arresting sight she must have been. Young. Blonde. Presumably virginal. He felt the jerk of some dark emotion he didn't want to analyse. 'You inspired him?' he asked slowly.

'I guess so. He wrote "Fairy Dancer" that same night. When it hit the top of the charts, he decided that I was his number-one muse and he couldn't live without me. That kind of thing can easily go to a young girl's head.' Especially when your mother was egging you on and telling you that you'd never get another chance quite like this one.

Louis had showered her with gifts and attention—and, more importantly, he hadn't leapt on her. He told her he respected her virginal status and that he would gladly wait until after they were married. And Emma had agreed, carried along on that unreal wave she was riding—as well as her mother's excitement. By the time her doubts had set in on the night before the wedding, it was too late. Her mother told her it was nothing but 'nerves' and to pull herself together.

'So I married him. And the rest of the story is well documented. I found him dead a year later from a combination of drink and drugs. It's not something I care to dwell on. Anything else you want to know, Mr Constantinides?'

Unexpectedly, he said, 'I thought I told you to call me Zak.'

She stared at him, shaken by the emotional catharsis of recounting a story which she'd buried deeply, want-

ing to tell him that calling him by his first name seemed
ridiculously intimate. That she wanted to keep as much
distance between them as possible. *Because something
about him was making her feel stuff. The sort of stuff
she was scared to feel because it was what had made
her mother's life such a mess. Desire and lust and a
yearning to be kissed. A longing to be loved and cher-
ished and made to feel the centre of someone's world.*
And yet, if she told him that—wouldn't she look hopelessly vulnerable as well as a hopeless judge of men?

'I'm very tired, *Zak.* How's that?'

'Better.'

'And I think I want to go to bed now.'

'But you haven't touched your meal.'

'Neither have you.'

'No.' Once again, Zak stared at his plate. Never had
a steak seemed more unappetizing, but then he'd never
found himself in a situation such as this. Parts of her
story had aroused in him an unwilling empathy and yet
that didn't change the fundamental problem. It didn't
matter that she had turned her life around—she had
done that mainly because she aroused fierce passions
in very rich men. Bottom line was that she was still the
wrong kind of woman for Nat and she always would be.

'I'll see you up to your room,' he said abruptly.

'There's no need.'

'There's every need,' he argued. 'You're jet-lagged
and probably feeling disorientated.'

She certainly was—but her disorientation wasn't
being helped by the fact that he was there. That the
closeness of his powerful body was taunting her with

the elusive promise of pleasure. And it was wrong for all kinds of reasons. Wrong because of Nat and wrong because it was Zak.

Weariness swept over her—a potent combination of not enough sleep or food, with a glass of rich red wine thrown in to further complicate it. Her body felt drained and her legs were shaky as they walked to the elevator, which was fortunately busy enough to preclude any kind of conversation. The lift doors opened on to the thirty-second floor and Zak followed her out, but as she reached her room and began to fumble in her bag for her key-card she felt herself stumble slightly. Felt Zak's hand automatically reach out to steady her and Emma stiffened as he gripped her.

His fingers seemed to sizzle through the thin material of her floaty top—almost as if they were scorching the skin which lay beneath. She could feel the thready patter of her heart and her breathing suddenly became as laboured as if she'd been running.

For a moment they stared into each other's eyes as time and place merged, the background of his fancy hotel blurring into insignificance so that all she could see was the darkened pewter of his burning gaze. And in that moment she wanted him. Wanted him in a way which wiped all reason from her sleep-deprived brain.

'Zak,' she whispered, although she didn't know why she said it—and, in view of her reluctance to say it earlier, it now seemed like an intimacy too far.

Zak heard the soft temptation of her voice and a powerful desire washed over him. *Let her go*, he urged himself savagely—but his body stubbornly refused to obey. Still his hand gripped the slim column of her arm and he was loath to pull his fingers away from the softness of her flesh.

He looked down at her, mesmerised by her closeness and the way she was looking at him. Her green eyes had grown smoky and her lips had parted in unconscious invitation and he knew that if he were to dip his head, he could claim them in a kiss which would combust. He imagined pulling her hungrily into his arms. The jut of his hips against hers and the silent circling of his heavy erection against her feminine softness. The urgent journey to her room and then the discarding of clothes until he felt her naked against him.

He could hear the powerful beat of his heart as the idea became a tantalising possibility and he could almost *taste* the desire which hovered in the air around them. She would let him do it. He *knew* she would. She would part her thighs and urge him into her sweet, molten tightness. Sweet heaven. Should he take her? *Should* he?

The vivid images playing in his head were almost his undoing until he forced himself to picture the sordid aftermath of such a coupling. Of confessing to his brother what he had done. Of having to look into her cheating face the next morning. He let his hand fall to his side, self-disgust hardening his lips into a savage line of contempt, appalled at his own weakness.

Was this how she had lured Louis Patterson? And then Ciro D'Angelo? And after that his brother? Like an earth-bound siren who could captivate men with her pale eyes and hair and the promise of her soft, curvy body?

He took a step back. 'You said you were tired,' he said harshly. 'In which case, I've always found it better to go to bed on your own.'

And with that, he turned on his heel—leaving Emma staring after him, her lips trembling as she registered his withering contempt. Aware that she had been chastised for something she hadn't even realised she'd been doing.

CHAPTER SIX

THE next morning Emma found an envelope shoved underneath her door and knew who it was from, even before she'd opened it. The stark black words seemed to leap off the expensive cream paper as her trembling fingers ripped it open.

"We neglected to talk about your work last night. Meet me in the lobby at ten. Zak."

And that was it. No endearment. No polite wishes expressed that he hoped she'd had a comfortable night. Which of course, she hadn't. The long hours of travel hadn't helped at all, and she'd woken at four thirty absolutely buzzing and unable to get back to sleep. She'd lain staring at the unfamiliar room and remembering those strange and provocative moments in the corridor, when she could have sworn that Zak was about to kiss her. When she'd *wanted him to kiss her.* And that had only been the beginning of what she'd wanted— she who had sworn off men and all the bitter fall-out of emotional attachment.

Had she gone completely crazy last night—or had she just been suffering from the potency of jet lag and wine? Opening up the blinds, Emma stared out of the window at the green oasis of Central Park. Either way, she wouldn't be making a fool of herself by repeating it.

Putting Zak's note down on the dresser, she showered and dressed—and ordered breakfast from room service. She crunched her way through toast and jam, forcing the food down because she knew she needed it, rather than because she really wanted it. But at least the coffee was good and strong and afterwards she felt much better.

But she was nervous when she arrived in the lobby and more nervous still when she saw Zak with his back to her, standing talking into his cellphone. How she hated the fact that her nerve-endings prickled into life when she saw him—when all she wanted to feel towards him was a cool impartiality. He was wearing a steel-grey suit and she was suddenly glad that she'd pulled something smarter from her wardrobe. She got the feeling that, in this city, clothes meant business.

He turned and saw her, terminating his call in a couple of brief words. His grey eyes narrowing, they scanned her with unwilling assessment.

Emma wondered what he saw. Had she failed on the sartorial front again? she wondered. Were a new sweater and pale jeans—stretchy enough for any ladder-climbing—still a little on the casual side for the wealthy hotelier's taste? He was coming towards her now and it was impossible to read his thoughts from his expression. The pewter eyes were shaded by thick black lashes and his rugged olive features were as hard as marble.

To Emma's embarrassment, her own colour had

started to rise—along with the realisation that the cold light of day had done nothing to lessen her desire for him. That last night had not been some erotic, one-off blip.

But now she had to act normally. As if she hadn't poured out her life-story to him over dinner last night and let the daylight in on the shadowy world of her past.

'Good morning,' she said, summoning up the brightest smile from her repertoire.

Zak noted the dark shadows beneath her eyes, which were at odds with the studiedly cheerful note in her voice. 'You look tired,' he observed.

'That's because I am.'

'Been emailing my brother all night, I suppose?' he enquired caustically.

Emma thought he couldn't have been further from the truth if he'd tried—why, she'd barely thought about Nat since the moment she'd arrived.

'Actually, no. I wasn't.' Because what on earth would she have said? *I'm sorry, Nat—I know I said that he was a tyrant and a control-freak, but last night I was longing for your brother to make love to me. I lay there waiting in my bed, imagining what I would do if he came to me, knowing that I would have opened the door and opened my arms to him.* 'I was too busy counting sheep to try to get to sleep,' she said hurriedly. 'But sadly, to no avail. So you'll have to excuse any absent-mindedness and blame it on the jet lag.'

Some of the tension left his body, her words placating him in a way they shouldn't have done. Had he been worried she'd tell Nat that his big brother had been coming on to her? And hadn't an extra layer of guilt begun to gnaw away at him, knowing that it would have been the truth? 'Have you eaten?' he questioned.

'Yes, thanks. I had breakfast in my room.' She smiled again, determined to dispel this damned *atmosphere* with a little professional crispness. 'It's a beautiful autumn morning and I'm looking forward to my first working day in New York! And you still haven't told me anything about which part of the hotel needs restyling.'

Her smile did strange things to him. Made that damned heaviness start throbbing at his groin again. He'd lain awake for a long time last night, going over what she'd told him about her growing up. About her flighty mother and the dancing which had angered the neighbours. He'd wanted to think less of her—but the stupid thing was that her story had produced the opposite effect. He'd thought about the reality of what her young life must have been like and had found himself experiencing a reluctant tug of sympathy. What Emma had experienced had been nothing short of neglect, he realised—some people might even have called it abuse. Somehow it made her early marriage to the dissolute rock-star almost understandable.

Until he told himself fiercely that this was how she operated. She knew exactly what she was doing. Her marriage to Patterson would have given her an inkling of her own power and taught her that such fragile beauty was rare. With that pale waterfall of hair and amazing body, she must have quickly learnt what effect that delicate vulnerability could have on a man. Especially a man with all the clout to protect her. Had she told

Ciro her pathetic story the way she'd told him—and had that been what had prompted the ruthless Italian to give her such a cushy job? Was that what had made his own brother curtail his philandering ways after all these years of messing around with women—to devote himself to her so wholeheartedly?

Zak's mouth hardened. Well, she could use her charm on some other poor sucker than Nat—because there was no way that some illegitimate junkie's widow was going to end up marrying into the Constantinides family.

'Come with me,' he said abruptly, turning as he began to walk in the direction of the function rooms, obviously expecting her to follow him.

Emma tried to take in the general mood and feel of the hotel as she scurried to keep up with him. She'd done her homework on the plane over by studying all the literature—but seeing the Pembroke's interior for herself was much more impressive than in the glossy pages of a brochure.

The Granchester was massive—but this hotel was like its small and perfectly formed little sister. Its understated elegance only reinforced the amount of money which must have been spent on it—and she found herself wondering if all this had been inherited from his wealthy father. Hadn't Nat told her some complicated story about the family money, which had gone in one ear and then out the other? And hadn't that been one of the things which had been so obvious to Nat—that she truly wasn't interested in the might of the Constantinides fortune? She sighed. Not that Zak would ever believe that, of course.

'This is the room you will be restyling,' he said, stopping at last in front of some art-deco double doors, which were decorated with exquisite stained glass. He pushed them open and Emma stepped into a room that was almost completely empty—but who needed furniture when a room looked as amazing as this? The proportions were generous, the high ceiling a shimmer of silver mosaic which looked as if it were composed of moving water—and best of all was the terrace, with its stunning views of Central Park and the quiet gleam of the lake beyond.

'Oh, Zak—it's lovely,' she said, looking up to find his eyes fixed on her. And something in that hard and searching gaze made her quickly amend her words—as if suddenly she wanted to encourage him to revise his poor opinion of her. 'I'm sorry, that's right up there as the most unoriginal observation I could have made. Of course it's lovely. You don't need me to tell you that.'

'No, I don't—though it's always gratifying when a professional approves.' For a moment, he relaxed a little. 'This is the room you'll be working on.'

'And do I get help?'

'You do. You'll get an assistant and an office you can use, as well as a charge card.'

'And I run my costs past…?'

'No need to run them past anyone.'

She looked at him in surprise. 'Really?'

He shrugged. 'I've seen your Granchester budgets. Since I note that you have an admirably frugal outlook, I'll give you a free hand.'

Stupidly pleased by this small sign of trust, Emma

smiled. 'And hadn't you better tell me what you're planning to do with it—what kind of vision you have for it?'

His answer was the last thing Emma was expecting to hear.

'I want to turn it into a wedding venue.'

'A wedding venue,' she repeated slowly.

'You sound surprised.'

'That's because I am.'

He slanted her a glance. 'And why is that, I wonder?'

She looked at him, tempted to be honest and yet, why *shouldn't* she be honest? What was the worst thing that could happen—that he wouldn't like plain speaking and send her home? She shrugged. 'You don't strike me as the kind of man who's particularly interested in weddings.'

'Show me any man who really is,' he said acidly. 'But there's a huge market for them—particularly here. Guests who stay here want to tie the knot here—they want the view and the glamour. Up until now I've always resisted—because, frankly, the attendant publicity is always a bore. And weddings seem to breed a hysteria in the female of the species which I can do without.'

She saw the cynical twist of his lips. 'But something's happened to change your mind?'

'Not something. Someone.'

'Someone?' she echoed, her heart pounding. 'Wh-who?'

He didn't appear to notice the stumbling of her voice. 'Her name is Leda.'

Emma screwed up her eyes, wondering why the name sounded familiar until she remembered where she'd heard it before. Leda was the name of the woman she'd seen him dining with, back in England. The woman with the dark, dramatic hair and amazing cheekbones.

'That's the woman you were with in London? The one in the miniskirt with the thigh-high boots?'

'That's the one.'

'She's getting…married?' she questioned faintly and suddenly she wondered if she'd read it all wrong. Was Zak about to marry the stunning woman who'd been his date? And if that was the case, then why no huge sense of relief that the tricky billionaire would soon be settling down and might therefore stop interfering in the life of his brother? Why was her instinctive feeling one of *jealousy*—a terrible, debilitating jealousy, which made her fingers curl into two tight little fists by her sides? Why did she suddenly want to open her mouth and scream? 'Who…who's she marrying?'

'Some banker from out of town.' He shrugged. 'He's a good guy, if a little on the unexciting side. But he'll make her happy.'

Emma looked into his pewter eyes and remembered something else. What had Nat said to him? *Everyone thought you two would get married.* Did Zak regret letting Leda go? Was he bitter about the fact that she was now about to marry the 'good guy'?

She turned her face up to his. 'This is a pretty wonderful thing you're doing for her,' she said quietly, her eyes searching for some kind of reaction.

'It's a commercial decision, not an emotional one,' he snapped.

Emma heard the hard note of finality in his voice and forced her attention back to the project, reminding herself that it was no business of hers even if he was still lusting after his ex-girlfriend. 'Did you have any particular ideas about what you wanted for the refurb?' she asked. 'Traditional or contemporary?'

He shook his head. 'Not my province,' he said as he glanced at his watch. 'I'm no expert and I'm not particularly interested. I assume you'll know the kind of things which prospective brides want and I'm giving you a free hand.'

Emma raised her eyebrows. 'It didn't occur to you that since I've been brought here under duress—I could completely sabotage your wedding room by making it all bubblegum pink and girly? Can you imagine how that would go down at the Pembroke? Why, the taste gurus would have a fit!'

He leaned forward and the musky tang of sandalwood once again invaded her senses.

'So they would. But that would be a very bad idea,' he warned softly. 'You see, people who cross me always live to regret it.'

She suspected he was referring to his brother and not bubblegum-pink walls, but his closeness was distracting.

'That sounds awfully like a threat,' she said quietly.

His lips curved into a smile. 'Not really. Just a quiet warning to let you know exactly where you stand.'

'I'd have to be pretty dense not to have realised that already. Tell me, do you always try to intimidate your staff?'

'Only the ones who give me trouble—but they are

few and far between and I don't generally tolerate them for very long.'

'So if I told you that I found your attitude insufferable and that I didn't want to work for you?'

'I'd be delighted.' His eyes gleamed. 'So delighted that I'd be tempted to give you a year's salary in lieu of notice.'

And he would have won, Emma realised. He would have achieved what he'd wanted to do all along. He would have managed to get rid of her without having to sack her—and she would have let Nat down.

'You really are a brute,' she accused crossly.

'I've never denied that. But most women seem to enjoy the way I treat them.'

'Are you so sure of that?'

'Put it this way—I've never had any complaints.'

Emma saw his eyes darken as their gazes clashed. Saw the tiny muscle flickering at the olive skin of his temple and the subsequent hardening of his mouth, as if he regretted his undeniably flirtatious words. But he couldn't take them back, could he? Nor could he dispel the darkly erotic images they had provoked.

And suddenly she wanted to lash out. She wanted to tell him to stop making her feel this way. As if she would do anything to have him take her in his arms and have him kiss away the unbearable tension which was building and building inside her. She could see the tension in his own big body and she wondered what might have happened next had not a bouncy little brunette entered the room.

'Hey, Zak!' said the brunette breezily, stopping dead

when she saw their frozen pose and looking uncertainly from one to the other. 'Oh, I'm sorry,' she said. 'Am I interrupting something?'

Quickly, Zak stepped away from Emma, his heart pounding as he forced himself to acknowledge just how close he'd been to taking her in his arms. Would he have kissed her? *Would* he? Even though she was his brother's woman—would he have been disloyal enough to lick his way into her soft, trembling mouth?

Swallowing down the unbearable combination of guilt and frustration, he forced himself to smile at the new arrival, even though smiling was the last thing he felt like doing. 'No, Cindy—you're not interrupting anything. This is Emma Geary, the interior designer from the Granchester we've been expecting. Emma and I were just establishing something fundamental, weren't we, Emma?' *And that something was that his brother had fallen for a woman who it seemed would put out for just about anyone with a Y chromosome and a bulging wallet!*

Emma heard the unmistakable edge of contempt in his voice and thought how unjust it was. He made her feel *cheap*. As if she'd done something wrong. Yet the sizzling attraction which had flowed between them had happened because he'd been flirting with her, boasting about his success with women. She hadn't provoked it— so why the hell should she be blamed for it? Realising that Cindy was still looking bemused, she reached out to shake the girl's hand, aware of the faint tremble of her own fingers.

'Yes, we were just establishing what an exacting man

Mr Constantinides can be to work for, but no doubt I'll learn to cope with all his idiosyncrasies! Any tips on how best to deal with him will be gratefully received.' She smiled. 'In the meantime, I'm very pleased to meet you, Cindy. We're going to make this the most sought-after place in the city for marriages—and I'm relying on you to introduce me to New York's best-kept design secrets.'

'Happy to do that,' beamed Cindy.

'I'll leave you in Cindy's capable hands,' said Zak, his cool voice completely at odds with the frustration eating him up inside. How dared she slant him that supercilious and dismissive look? 'I'll look in from time to time for an update. Anything you want, or need—just speak to one of my assistants.'

Emma should have been glad that he was leaving. Relieved that her body would be free of the tantalising distraction he represented. So why the sudden heart-sink? Aware of Cindy's curious eyes on her, she nodded and tried to match his careless tone. 'Right. I'll see you around.'

'I can hardly wait,' he murmured.

His sarcastic aside was so soft that Emma realised it had floated right over Cindy's head—but then, Cindy hadn't seen the unsettling look which was glittering from his cold grey eyes.

CHAPTER SEVEN

'So have you decided which one you're going with, Emma?'

Emma blinked, aware from the expression on her assistant's face that Cindy must have just asked her a question, but not quite sure what that question had been. 'Sorry?' she questioned, hating her current butterfly grip on reality. 'I was…I was miles away.'

'So I can see!' Cindy gestured towards the huge windows. 'I was asking whether you'd decided on the silk or the voile drapes?'

Emma forced herself to concentrate on the medley of fabrics which were lying on the table in front of her. 'Oh, definitely the off-white Belgian linen. It'll let the light in and it's suitably…' she gave Cindy a weak smile '…bridal.'

She bent her head to consult her long to-do list, wondering what the hell was happening to her. Losing herself in her current project had been one of the things she most loved about her job. She liked the aspect of designing a room which took you out of yourself and into another world, one you'd created all on your own.

She'd seen her mother do it time and time again, transforming the windows of yet another grim rental property with filmy material she'd bought cheap at the market. It had been one of her more admirable traits— her refusal to be beaten down by poverty. Her mother had shown that you didn't need to spend a fortune to improve your environment, and that sense of wonder and transformation had never left Emma. Immersing herself completely in her work was usually enough to make the minor problems of life seem fairly unimportant.

But not this time.

This time she felt like someone who'd suffered a bee-sting and been left with an allergic reaction which wouldn't go away. She couldn't stop thinking about Zak. About the physical aching he'd awoken in her—with nothing more than a fleeting touch accompanied by a dark and brooding stare. Was she really so lacking in judgment and experience that an innocuous touch like that would waken all kinds of longing?

She'd told him about Louis, too—more than she usually told anyone. Why had she done that? Because he'd asked all the right questions, or because—as her boss— he'd been holding most of the power? Either way, it had worked.

At least Cindy was sparky and energetic enough not to notice her occasional lapse into silence—which usually followed one of Zak's rare visits to see how work on the wedding room was progressing.

In truth, it was progressing very well—but then, Emma was discovering that New York was a very efficient city and that this time around she was seeing a completely different side to it. The darkened hotel rooms from which Louis wouldn't emerge until mid-day were firmly in the past. Waking up to the spill and smell of half-eaten food was a memory she was happy to leave behind.

Instead, she found herself up bright and early, traipsing around the sidewalks with Cindy, wrapped up warmly against the crisp autumn breeze. Together, they went scouting for antiques on Broadway and 10th and 11th, while for more contemporary pieces they ventured down to Soho and Chelsea. She learned to love the buzz of the city and the clean, wide streets, which were so easy to negotiate.

To her surprise, she'd heard nothing from Nat—apart from a couple of text messages soon after she'd first arrived. His phone went straight through to voicemail and he hadn't answered her email. She wondered if that meant he'd met someone new…

One morning, she was sitting on the terrace making notes on table settings when a soft footfall disturbed her, and she looked up to see Zak standing there.

Be professional, she urged herself, hating the hammering of her heart as she curved her mouth into a polite smile.

'Zak, this is a—'

'Pleasant surprise?' he finished sardonically.

She shrugged. Was she going to carry on pretending she hadn't noticed he'd been avoiding her—or was she going to do the adult thing and try to clear the air? 'Well, that's up to you, surely? You can carry on playing the big boss-man who can't bear to be in the same room as me—or you could try getting along with me.'

He stepped out onto the terrace to join her, where the breeze held in it the first faint chill of winter—despite the brightness of the sun. He looked down at her. She was sitting bundled up in jeans and a jacket, her hair piled high on her head—her face completely bare of make-up. He noticed that today her fingernails were painted pale lemon, which matched the filmy scarf she wore looped around her neck. He'd never seen a woman with yellow nails before.

Pulling out a chair, he sat down next to her. 'Maybe you're right.'

'He said grudgingly.' The glance she shot him was enough to establish that his shirt was fine—silk probably—and that she could see the faint outline of his torso through it. 'You'll get cold out here without a jacket.'

He raised his eyebrows. 'It might come as a surprise for you to learn that somehow, despite the lack of your intervention, I've managed to survive a whole thirty-six years without ever getting pneumonia.'

She rested her pen on her notepad. 'Are you always this defensive?'

Zak turned his head to look at the park. Not always, no. But then, his relationships with women were usually clearly demarcated. There were women he did business with and women who worked for him. There were women he had relationships with—admittedly rare. And then there were the women he slept with—which had always happened whenever he had wanted it to happen. There had never been a woman he'd wanted that he couldn't have.

Until now.

Behind the indifference of his smile, his teeth clamped together in frustration. Because wasn't the truth that he wanted Emma Geary with a hunger which was eating away at him? That thoughts of her kept him awake at night—awake and hard and bathed in a sweat which cold showers seemed only momentarily to subdue. It didn't seem to matter that her background appalled the fiercely proud side of his Greek nature—or that she was involved with his brother. His betraying body still jerked into instant life whenever he thought of that waterfall of pale hair and those strange green eyes. When he imagined her painted fingernails tiptoeing over the heated arousal of his flesh.

'You seem to bring out the worst in me, Emma.'

'And why's that, I wonder? Because I'm not docile enough to accept everything you say as law?'

He turned his head to look at her and gave a reluctant shrug. 'There's definitely an element of that. Your defiance is a little…unusual,' he conceded.

'You mean women don't usually answer you back?'

'They don't usually feel a need to, no.'

'Because you're always "right", I suppose?'

'It's a little more complex than that.' His eyes gleamed. 'Don't you know that, deep down, all women crave a masterful man?'

She shook her head, glad that the wind was chilly enough to cool the sudden heat in her cheeks. When he looked at her that way, it was difficult not to agree with him even when he was spouting out such ridiculously old-fashioned sentiments. 'You must mix in some very strange circles to think that way, Zak.'

'Possibly.' Leaning back in the chair, he saw that the trees in the park were almost bare. Soon it would be winter, and holiday time. The big Christmas tree would go up at the Rockefeller Center and tourists and New Yorkers would ice-skate side by side in the dazzle of its lights. Emma would complete her assignment here and she would go back to London—and to Nat. Zak's mouth hardened as he forced himself to confront a scenario he had managed to suppress until now. Because what if his plan failed? What if, despite his intervention, she went back and married his brother. What then?

He had always looked out for Nat. Been there for him when nobody else was and his love for his brother burned fiercely in his heart. But sometimes events had a habit of running away with themselves. Didn't matter how hard you tried, you couldn't always determine the outcome. He remembered his mother lying sobbing on the marble floor and the sound of the door slamming as his father walked out of their lives. He hadn't been able to prevent *that*, had he?

Suddenly, and with disturbing clarity, he could picture Emma as Nat's new bride—her long blond hair blowing in the breeze. The image intensified and he could even imagine her dress—one of those long, filmy things which foreign girls always wore when they went to Greece, her feet bare with the blue of the Mediterranean dancing behind her. Maybe she would give Nat hordes of children who would, along with her, become part of his family and therefore linked to him for life. And if that happened, he would have to kill his desire for her stone-dead—or risk severing his relationship with his only brother.

And wouldn't the way to do that be by engaging with her, no matter how uncomfortable he might initially find it? Couldn't they form an uneasy truce in case the worst *did* happen? At the moment she symbolised the tantalising and the forbidden—and that only increased her desirability. Shouldn't he give her the opportunity to spend the evening chattering idly about nothing, as women so often did? Wouldn't the subsequent tedium of such an encounter assure him that she was nothing special after all?

Unexpectedly, he found himself asking, 'Have you seen much of the city?'

Surprised by his question, Emma nodded. 'Actually, I have.' She'd decided that she wasn't going to sit around moping—but to explore a place she'd seen remarkably little of last time around. So she'd taken a tour-bus and giggled at the native New Yorker's rumbustious commentary as they passed all the iconic buildings. She'd worked her way through all the art galleries and walked daily in Central Park. And she'd taken the ferry to Staten Island, where she'd eaten a hot dog nearly as long as her arm. 'I've done all the must-see touristy things.'

He stopped looking at the park and gave in to the temptation of studying her face. 'So I can't persuade you to have dinner with me tonight?'

Emma's fingers tightened around the pen she was

still holding. 'And why would I want to do that? More to the point, why would *you*?'

He smiled at her frankness. 'Maybe I've decided I should get to know you a little better if my evil plan doesn't work and you do end up becoming my sister-in-law.'

Emma shoved the pen deep into the pocket of her jacket, acknowledging that his careless smile was potent. Very potent. It humanised him and made him seem gloriously accessible—so that she stupidly found herself wanting to reach up and trace the sensual curve of his lips with her finger.

Eaten up with a terrible feeling of remorse, she knew this was the moment to come clean. To tell him that this was all a game—and that there was nothing romantic between her and his brother. But something stopped her and she wasn't sure if it was fear of his reaction—or because she'd convinced herself that she needed to warn Nat first.

And if she *didn't* tell him, then how could she possibly refuse an invitation which sounded like an attempt at reconciliation?

'What kind of dinner?' she questioned suspiciously.

'You can lose the look of horror—I'm not suggesting a cosy meal for two in some candlelit restaurant. I have a duty dinner on the other side of the city. You can be my partner for the evening, if you like.'

What could she say? That she was scared of accompanying him anywhere because he made her feel so...so *vulnerable*? She shrugged. 'Okay,' she said cautiously.

'Okay?' His eyes narrowed. 'Is that it? I've had more enthusiastic responses from a water-cooler.'

'You're in the habit of inviting water-coolers out to dinner?'

He gave the glimmer of a smile. 'Very funny.'

'I do my best.' She tried to tell her stupid heart to stop slamming so wildly against her ribcage, but it didn't work because Emma recognised that a brief moment of humour was as intoxicating as strong liquor. 'Will it be dressy?'

'It will. Black tie and long dresses. I'll order a car—so meet me in the lobby at eight.'

'Eight it is.'

Emma's heart was still racing as she searched her wardrobe for something suitable to wear, finding fault in every single item she pulled out. Within half an hour she was outside on the busy sidewalk, knowing that she wanted to buy something new and not daring to question why she didn't just make do with something she already had.

But it was a long time since Emma had shopped for clothes and she felt an unfamiliar excitement as she scoured the fancy shops on Madison Avenue. The stores were packed with gorgeous garments, but something made her steer away from the rails of safe and staple black. Instead, she was drawn to a white silk dress which was draped and pleated in all the right places and fell in soft folds to the ground. She didn't need any pressure from the cooing saleswoman to buy it, though when she put it on in her hotel room a couple of hours later she started to have second thoughts about her purchase. Was she showing too much flesh? Was it sending out the wrong kind of message?

The expression in Zak's eyes when she walked into the crowded lobby only intensified her feeling of nervousness.

'It isn't suitable?' she questioned, a note of vulnerability creeping into her voice as she saw the sudden narrowing of his eyes.

Suitable? Zak's mouth dried as his gaze drifted over her. Her arms were bare and the dress was cut low, the soft white silk moulding her breasts and skimming the curve of her hips as it fell to the floor. The long tumble of her pale hair flowed down over her shoulders like liquid moonlight. She looked, he thought suddenly, like a Greek goddess. A perfect statue who had come to life for one night only. He must have been out of his *mind* to propose taking her to dinner.

'Oh, it's suitable all right,' he said, in an odd kind of voice as he led the way to the waiting car. 'But I'm probably going to spend the entire evening playing bodyguard.'

She raised her eyebrows. 'Though maybe from your boasts of earlier and all the things I've heard about your legendary success with women—perhaps it's me who'll have to play bodyguard to you?'

'You really think you could fight them off, do you, Emma?'

She met the challenge in his eyes. 'I could try.'

He shifted his weight, distracted by the way she had crossed her leg, so that the white silk was now clinging to one shapely thigh like rich cream. 'Then I'd better put out a general alert that all women should tonight keep their distance.'

The lazy note in his voice made Emma's breasts tighten and she wanted to tell him to stop being so *nice* to her. Or, more to the point, to stop flirting with her. This was crazy. How was she going to endure the rest of the evening when he had the power to make her feel like *this*?

'So whose party is it?' she asked, in an attempt to change the subject.

With difficulty, he averted his gaze from the pin-pointing of her nipples against the white silk. 'An old friend of my father's. His granddaughter, Sofia, is twenty-one—and he's giving her a coming-of-age party.'

Emma nodded, remembering something Nat had said. 'Nat told me that your father had died last year. I'm…well, I'm sorry, Zak.'

For a moment he said nothing, realising that his brother must have told her about all kinds of things—resenting the fact that he couldn't control the flow of information. That this woman probably knew more about him than most people. More than he wanted her to know. How much had he told her?

'Thanks,' he said tersely.

'I understand he was ill for a long time.'

Which answered his question. She knew plenty. 'Thanks again,' he said, just as tersely.

Hearing his abrupt sense of closure, Emma looked out of the window and watched the night-time city slide past. The big car weaved its way through the busy streets, before coming to a halt at the front of a glittering hotel, whose arching entrance was garlanded with pink and white blooms.

Emma became aware of the press standing waiting outside and of Zak's terse exclamation when he saw them—but this was something she was an old hand at dealing with. Dipping her head so that her hair fell like a mantle to obscure her face, she was inside the building before any of the intrusive flashes could capture her face for posterity, with Zak close behind her, and when she turned round she saw that he was laughing.

'That's the first time a woman's ever *avoided* being photographed with me!'

'You think I want to be seen with *you*?'

'I hadn't thought of that.'

But her modesty and rejection of publicity pleased him inordinately, and forced him to confront his initial prejudices. Would she really be such a bad choice of woman for his brother, if she made him happy? Once he got to know her a little better, wouldn't this inconvenient lust for her simply melt away?

Emma was aware of him guiding her through to the grand ballroom where the party was being held. The room was decked out in the same pink and white roses they'd seen outside and there were matching balloons and sugared almonds at every place setting. It was a bit cheesy, but somehow it worked—especially when a slender, dark-haired girl in a pink voile dress came running up to Zak and flung her arms around him.

'Thios Zakharias!' she bubbled enthusiastically. 'I'm so glad you came—and thank you for my earrings!'

He smiled. 'You like them?'

'I love them! See? I'm wearing them now!' She pushed back her heavy black hair to reveal two creamy pearl studs. 'Come and have a drink. Grandfather is around somewhere and so is Mama. Oh, and there's Loukas—I must go and say hello!'

Emma felt suddenly a little shy to find herself in the middle of such a large and lively party. She could hear bursts of laughter and snatches of incomprehensible Greek and as she looked around she thought that she'd never been in a group of people who were quite so *animated*.

'Everyone seems to be having a great time,' she observed.

'If there's one thing a Greek knows how to do, it's party.'

At his words, Emma's nerves fled and, despite the rather bizarre circumstances which had brought about this pairing, she began to enjoy herself. And so did Zak, playing the part of attentive partner perfectly. He introduced her to lots of people during the pre-dinner drinks and she struggled to remember all their names as they surveyed her with frankly curious eyes. He explained the history behind the food when they sat down to eat, because 'everything in Greece has a story,' and kept her entertained with stories about Sofia's grandfather's fabled exploits as a young man, when he had left his Greek island determined to make his fortune and had returned a millionaire.

It was the first time that Emma had been subjected to the full force of his charm and it was powerful stuff. It was only when the band came on and started playing that she began to feel awkward. Couples got up to dance, so that they were left alone at their table, and suddenly she felt like an outsider, as if she didn't really belong here. But then, she'd never really belonged anywhere, had she?

Zak's eyes narrowed. 'You look as if you've just heard the world will be ending in the next five minutes.'

She shrugged, trying to block out the lure of the music and her own sense of isolation. 'It's a bit *noisy*.'

'Well, we could try shouting to make ourselves heard— or we could just slip away. We've done our duty, I think.'

Which told her unequivocally just how he'd rated the evening. Emma looked at his rugged features and an unbearable temptation swept over her as she wondered what it would be like to dance with him—just once? Ignoring the warning bells which were screaming in her brain, she smiled—wondering if it was the wine or the music which made her words tumble out.

'There's another alternative,' she said, gesturing towards the parquet dance floor. 'We could always dance.'

Zak felt himself tense. It had been bad enough having to steel himself against the visual feast she made in her white silk dress. To have had to keep averting his eyes from the swell of her magnificent breasts. But dancing with her would be insane. Completely insane. There were a million reasons why they shouldn't do it and yet the thought of being able to hold her in his arms swept every single one of them away. What harm could one dance do?

'Then let's do it,' he murmured, getting to his feet.

She took the hand he offered her and followed him on to the dance floor, but it was only when she was standing in front of him that she became properly aware of his towering height. The feel of his hands on her waist made her feel tiny and her nose only just reached to the top of his shoulder. This close, his scent was more defined—a tantalising mixture of sandalwood combined with warm, male flesh, which crept over her senses.

She could hear the hypnotic note of a single instrument above the rest of the music, an unfamiliar sound which tugged at her heartstrings. 'I love that sound,' she said.

'The bouzouki? I love it, too. Some people think it's corny—but it's traditionally Greek.'

And so was he, she thought, her palms spreading luxuriously over his shoulders as their bodies moved in perfect time. Like someone you'd see on the front of a coin—he was pure and unadulterated alpha male.

Zak could feel the sway of her hips and the silken brush of her hair against his cheek. She danced like a dream, he thought. He closed his eyes. Of course she did. It was a particular skill and one which her mother had taught her. He'd forgotten that when he'd agreed to this.

Suddenly he could understand why a man could be driven half mad with desire by watching her. Why some aging rock-star had been captivated by her. Her breasts were brushing against him and he could feel their diamond tips against his chest—or was that simply fevered fantasy on his part?

Either way, he was getting so aroused that he could barely move without giving himself away. His mouth twisted as he registered the near-painful ache of his erection and he was suddenly filled with a feeling of disgust. What kind of man was so turned on by his brother's woman that he could have pulled her into the nearest darkened alcove and ravished her while the sounds of the party went on in the background?

He had to stop this and to stop it now. He must have been out of his *mind* to think that he could dance with her and not want her. Abruptly removing his hands from her waist, he dipped his head to her ear, so that his words could be heard above the hypnotic lull of the music.

'Let's go,' he clipped out.

'Go?' She turned her face up to his. 'But we've only just started dancing.'

And in that moment, all the pretence he'd been maintaining and the defences he'd erected came tumbling down and desire transmuted into a quiet and burning rage. 'I don't know if you're being naïve or disingenuous, Emma—but we can't keep doing this,' he hissed. 'All this crazy flirting and touching and denying ourselves what we both really want. *Because it's wrong.* We both know it's wrong. And sooner or later, we're just not going to be able to stop ourselves. You might find it acceptable to have two men on the go— but I won't do it. I may want you, but I can't have you.

If you want the truth, there's part of me which despises your siren ways even as I'm sucked in by them. And the thought that you've woven your spell around my poor, unsuspecting brother makes me sick to my stomach.'

She heard the venom in his voice as his accusation cut through her and she knew that she had to tell him. That maybe she should have told him a long time ago.

'B-but I haven't,' she stumbled. 'You've got it all wrong. There's nothing between me and Nat and there never has been.'

He froze. 'What the hell are you talking about?'

'We're just good friends,' she explained, her words coming out in a babble in their eagerness to be spoken. 'I played along with the idea of you separating us because he thought it would get you off his back for a while. He was fed up with you always playing the big, controlling brother—and he thought it'd do me good to come to New York. That's all.'

'That's *all*?' A pulse beat at Zak's temple as what she'd just told him began to sink in. He'd endured days of guilt and long, sleepless nights of frustration—and she thought she could shrug it off with an insouciant 'that's all'? A bitter anger crept over him. 'We're going,' he bit out as he caught hold of her wrist and led her off the dance floor.

The expression on his face was dark and formidable and Emma was aware of people watching them. Grabbing her bag from her chair, she shot a glance at his stony profile as they made their way towards the exit. 'Zak?'

'Shut up,' he gritted out, signalling for the doorman to have his car brought out to the front.

And they stepped out of the hotel to the blue-white flash of the waiting paparazzi.

CHAPTER EIGHT

'Zak?' Emma attempted for a second time as the car pulled away from the kerb.

'Shut up,' he gritted out again.

Her shoulders miserably tense, Emma sat upright in the luxury car while he brooded beside her in stony silence. What choice did she have but to obey him? She guessed she could jump out of the limousine when they stopped at a light. She could run down the road and hail a cab—but wouldn't that only add to the general melodrama of the evening and make it even worse? Clutching at her little gold clutch bag, she could feel mounting frustration at her own stupidity.

Why the hell hadn't she told him about Nat sooner—way back when? She'd known that there was some sort of *chemistry* between them right from the start. She'd known that they had both been fighting an unwanted and very physical attraction. So why had she just pretended that it wasn't happening—until it had combusted in that steamy dance at the party and it had been impossible to hide from the truth any longer? And now he was angry with her—she didn't think she'd ever seen anyone so angry.

The car stopped outside the Pembroke and she half expected Zak to storm off, but, still with that same grim look on his face, he led her through the lobby to the elevator, punching out her floor number with an angry finger. Within the closed confines of the empty lift, the atmosphere was unbearable and then suddenly he erupted, turning on her with pewter fire flashing from his eyes.

'Why did you do that?' he demanded, his voice low and fierce. 'Why did you lie about your relationship with my brother, knowing as you must have known that the attraction between us was growing all the time? Or was that what turned you on? Is that what you always do with men, Emma—watch them getting eaten up with desire until they can't help themselves? Did it amuse you to see me fighting the way I felt about you?'

'Of course it didn't!'

'So why the subterfuge? Why not just come straight out and tell me?'

She shook her head, not ready to tell him that she'd felt too vulnerable to tell him the truth. That she'd been *afraid* of the way she felt about him and the effect it'd had on her. In fact, she was still afraid. Hadn't her mother been made a fool of by men who were out of her reach, time and time again? And hadn't the debacle of her own disastrous marriage proved that Emma was formed from the same mould as the woman who had given birth to her?

'Because there never seemed a right time,' she

hedged. 'And because I'd promised Nat that I'd get you off his back.'

'If Nat had wanted that, then he should have had the guts to tell me so himself!' he flared. And then he shook his head, amazed at his own stupidity. If Nat had really loved Emma, then there was no way on earth he would have tolerated her being moved away to another city like that. Why hadn't he seen that before?

Because as usual he had been trying to fix things. To orchestrate events from the sidelines, the way he'd always done. A muscle worked in his cheek as he re-alised the full extent of his need to control. But he wasn't going to beat himself up about it. That was the way he'd had to be. Hadn't he needed every bit of that steely control, in order for his family to survive? When the Constantinides fortune had been bled away by his father's vacuous new wife—and his mother's conse-quent illness—hadn't Zak been the one that everyone had relied on?

He stared down at Emma, at the slanted green eyes and pale tumble of her hair. He'd been planning to leave her at her room and then to go back to his own, to maybe drink himself into oblivion and think about what a fool he'd been. But his eyes now focused on the soft white silk which clung to yet concealed the pale, curvy body beneath. And suddenly he thought, *What the hell?*

The lift doors slid open at her floor but as she made to exit, he caught hold of her wrist and pulled her back inside, so that she was wedged right up close to his chest.

'What do you think you're doing?' she whispered.

'Let's lose the innocent act, shall we? I'm going to do what you've been wanting me to do all night. I'm going to kiss you, Emma. To kiss you until you don't know where your mouth ends and mine begins—and after that I'm going to make love to you. Unless, of course, you don't want me to?' He read the darkened hunger in her eyes and saw the helpless tremble of her lips. 'No, I thought not,' he said grimly as he hit the button for the 34th floor. 'Because you want this just as much as me. You've wanted this from the first moment you ever set eyes on me. We both have. And now we're damned well going to *do it* and maybe then it'll stop eating away at me.'

He was all out of words and all out of excuses and, even though a part of him despised his own weakness, he drove his mouth onto hers in a kiss which had been a long time in coming.

Emma swayed as his mouth came down hard on hers and she found her lips opening greedily. Was this right or was this wrong? She didn't know—and right now she didn't care. Because there was no alternative. None. The thought of going through the rest of her life and not kissing him, of never experiencing this—would surely make it an empty life.

Her eyes fluttered to a helpless close as his hands splayed possessively over her bare back. It felt as if her body were melting and this wretched dress was burning her skin and she could barely wait for him to touch her properly. The sensation of it was so powerful that, for a moment, her knees buckled.

Yet even as her body felt on fire with need a part of

her found it hard to believe that this was really happening. Because she'd never had this feeling before. Not with Louis. Not with anyone. She'd thought it was her—that it was all down to her own inadequacy. Because that was the accusation which men hurled at women when they couldn't…couldn't…arouse them.

The lift stopped and the doors slid open to reveal a couple in full evening dress who were blinking at them in surprise.

'Good evening,' said Zak pleasantly as he caught Emma's hand and walked straight past them.

But Emma heard the woman's voice as it floated after them down the corridor.

'Did you *see* what they were doing, Earl?'

'I sure did,' answered Earl, an unmistakable trace of envy in his voice.

Emma's cheeks were flushed and her heart was pounding by the time they reached Zak's suite—but she was too nervous with excitement to give the vast penthouse more than a cursory look.

'I'm not going to offer you a drink,' he said. 'Because we both know we're not here for cocktails. There has been too much deception, Emma, and there's not going to be any more. Not tonight. Do you understand?'

She nodded. 'Yes.'

'Tonight we're going to be very honest with each other. You're going to tell me exactly what it is you want, and I'm going to give it to you.'

His words both thrilled her and scared her because how was she supposed to know what she wanted? How on earth could she tell him that she *didn't know*? Nerves momentarily threatened to overwhelm her, but then he had pulled her into his arms and was grazing his lips over hers and she began to shiver in helpless response.

'Zak,' she breathed as he flicked her lips open with the arrogant lick of his tongue and she could feel the warm mingling of their breath.

'Tell me, what is it you want, Emma?'

'I want…' Her words trailed away. How could she articulate what had only ever been a fantasy?

'This, perhaps?' His hand cupped her breast, luxuriantly circling the rocky nipple so that she moaned.

Against his shoulder, she squirmed with excitement, swallowing down the paper dryness in her throat. 'Yes,' she whispered.

'I thought so. Now let's try this…' His hand skated over her belly, his fingers drifting over the delicate silk-satin of her white dress until, with blatant possession, they rested at her crotch. Briefly, his fingers whispered over her sensitive mound, and he ignored her little gasp of protest as he drifted them further down to splay over her thigh.

'Zak,' she murmured brokenly, her eyes tightly shut, scared she was going to crumple to the carpet and give away just how useless she was at all this.

Assessingly, he ran his gaze over her as she clung to him, his heart beating with an excitement he hadn't felt in a long, long time. She was certainly very turned on. Enough for him to just push her down onto the carpet and do it to her right there—and part of him was angry enough at her deceit to want to do just that. To take her in as swift and as perfunctory a way as possible and then to get rid of her as fast as he could.

But even though it had been less than a month since he'd met her, he could never remember feeling quite like this before—as if he would die if he didn't possess her. Was that the power of the forbidden? Because for so long he'd thought he couldn't have her? What was it they said—that forbidden fruit was the sweetest? Yet through the dying waves of his anger he realised something else—something which was far more dangerous than acknowledging the allure of the forbidden. He didn't want it fast and furious, with him just unzipping his fly and thrusting into her eager flesh. If it was only going to be once, then it was going to last all night. One unforgettable night.

He picked her up with the minimum of effort, enjoying the way her eyes snapped open and registering her delighted gasp with a grim satisfaction. So she, who had expressed disbelief that women liked masterful men, was discovering that she'd been wrong all along, was she?

He carried her into the bedroom, where he set her down on her high heels and sucked in a deep breath while she steadied herself, her hands holding on to his shoulders.

'Take off your shoes,' he said.

He was so…so in control, she thought as, shakily, she bent down to slip each foot free. Without the added inches of the gold stilettos, she was suddenly much shorter, and once again a feeling of vulnerability swept over her—particularly when she heard his next comment.

'Is this dress new?'

'Yes.'

'So you bought it especially for me,' he mused, his lips hardening. 'That's interesting. Was it expensive?'

She shrugged. Did she look *foolish*, buying a new dress for what was supposed to have been an innocent date all along? Did it seem as if she'd been expecting this to happen all along? 'It was enough.'

'Then bill me for another,' he said savagely as he peeled it unceremoniously from her body and threw it to the floor, where it pooled in a silken white puddle. He shrugged off his dinner jacket, and it joined the dress on the floor, black against white—as stark as the contrast between his dark skin and her pale flesh. 'Now unzip me,' he commanded unsteadily.

The dark eroticism in his voice filled Emma with an urgency she'd never felt before. And once again the dizzy realisation hit her that this was how it was supposed to feel. As if nothing else in the world mattered at that moment other than what was taking place between this man and this woman.

Tremblingly, her fingers struggled with the zipper, which was straining against his hardness. She was terrified that she would ruin it. But he gave a groan of what sounded like satisfaction as his erection sprang free— though he clamped his fingers around hers when she attempted to stroke his steely length through the black silk of his boxer shorts.

'Don't,' he warned. 'Not this time. Just unbutton my shirt. Leave the rest to me.'

This time? What was he talking about? But there

wasn't time to think—not to do anything—because now Zak was removing his shoes and socks and kicking off his trousers and she was busy sliding free the buttons of the fancy dress shirt.

His hand skimmed its way down the side of her body as if he was learning her through touch alone and Emma was suddenly aware that they were both wearing nothing but their underwear. That she was standing in front of him in her bra and pants and that soon they would reach the part where it might go as hopelessly and as disastrously wrong as it had in the past. Would it? Would Zak Constantinides turn to her and snarl his frustration and his rage at her? Hotness flooded into her cheeks and he lifted her chin to meet the blaze of his eyes.

'Blushing?' he questioned in a thoughtful voice, his thumb tracing the curve of her jaw.

'It's all been a bit…sudden,' she prevaricated. 'It feels… fast.'

'If you want me to be slow, I'm not sure that I can.' His eyes narrowed. 'What *is* it you want from me, Emma?'

'I just…'

Her words tailed off because she was unsure of how to express herself. Even she knew that it would be madness to warn him that it might all go terribly wrong. *Because what if that made him stop?* So instead, she just spoke the words which came straight from her heart. The ones which were inspired by the desire she felt for this daunting and powerful man. 'I just want you to be you,' she breathed.

There was a brief pause. 'Oh, do you now?' His soft words to her were at odds with the hardening of his mouth. How like a woman, he thought bitterly. Couldn't she see the irony in what she'd said? That all this time she'd been deceiving him and now she had the temerity to make a breathless little request like that!

Through the beat of desire he felt another flicker of fury, but he sublimated it by concentrating on undressing her, recognising that rage would get in the way of his enjoyment. And one thing he was certain of was that he was going to enjoy this. *Theos*, but he had waited for it long enough!

He unclipped her strapless bra—a skimpy little thing, which was having to fight against gravity to contain her luscious breasts, and he was unable to stem his instinctive murmur of appreciation when they sprang free. Urgently, he turned his attention to a tiny white thong, which skimmed the pale curve of her hips and which he slid down over her thighs before kicking off his own shorts so that they were both naked. For a moment he sucked in a deep and unsteady breath, because this was happening—something he had never envisaged happening, other than in his tortured dreams.

Her pale green eyes looked blurred and he wondered if he imagined the faint wariness which lurked at their depths. And he knew that he didn't want her to have any doubts. That nothing was going to stop this. Not her. Not him. Nothing. He put his arms around her and dipped his face so that it was close to hers.

'You want this?' he questioned urgently.

'I do,' she whispered back.

With a small groan he tumbled them down on the bed as skin met skin, their bodies sinking into the deep mattress as his fingers threaded through the pale spill of her hair.

'Oh, Emma,' he groaned. 'Emma. I've dreamt of doing this. Every night, this has been my forbidden fantasy and now it's finally coming true.'

He kissed her lips. Her neck. The lobes of her ears. He kissed her until she made sweet little sounds in the back of her throat. Dragging his lips downwards to her breast, he weaved his tongue over the puckering pink of her nipple, his hand drifting irresistibly down over her belly towards the soft fuzz of hair at the juncture of her thighs.

'Zak!' she moaned as his hand moved to cup her intimately and all her shyness and fear was banished by the expert way he was strumming his fingers against her moist heat. Pleasure rushed through her in a warm, unstoppable stream. She could feel the powerful beat of his heart and smell the scent of her own arousal as her body thrilled to his touch. And something made her fingernails dig into his back—some urgent need to have more than this. To have Zak as close as it was possible for him to be. To see whether this time…

'Please…' she breathed.

Briefly, he released her—reaching out to the drawer in the antique locker next to the bed, until he had found what he was looking for.

He couldn't remember ever having quite so much difficulty slipping on a condom and it wasn't helped by Emma planting urgent little butterfly kisses all over his shoulders. But when he had sheathed himself he moved over her, savouring that last brief moment against her moist heat before he entered her long and hard and deep.

Her gasp was unlike any other he'd ever heard because wasn't it tinged with a note of what sounded like...*surprise*? He stilled as, briefly, he felt her stiffen.

'Emma?' Confusedly, he stared down at her, but she had now closed her eyes tight shut, her chin lifted upward—like a flower reaching for the sun. 'Emma?' he questioned again.

'Just make love to me, Zak,' she urged fervently against his warm damp skin. 'Please.'

His bewilderment was dissolved by that throaty little plea, his conscience appeased by the dig of her fingernails into his shoulders. With a moan, he began to move again, thrusting deep into her molten heat—his body so dark against the paleness of hers. Her mouth was on his and he held her close as their bodies rocked together in perfect rhythm. She was so *tight*, he thought as he deepened the kiss. Tighter than any woman he'd ever known.

He wanted to come. He'd wanted it from the moment he had entered her and never had it seemed so difficult to hold back. He felt as if he were a teenager. As if it were his first time. As if there had never been any other woman but her. *He wanted to come like never before!* But somehow he clung on until he heard the shudder of her breathing and felt the change in her body as it began to arch and then to splinter around his. And only then did he let go, spilling his seed in an orgasm which went on like no other, sending him orbiting into some crazy new dimension.

He clutched her still-shuddering body and buried his mouth in her silken hair. For a moment there was no sound in the room other than their ragged breathing and Zak wished he could just hold on to this feeling and turn over and go to sleep.

But he hadn't got this far in life by ignoring the screamingly obvious and he rolled off her and lay on his side, his eyes watchful as he stared at her flushed face and wary eyes.

'So, Emma,' he questioned unsteadily, 'was that some kind of erotic game-play done to heighten your enjoyment?' His grey eyes bored into her. 'Or could you really have been a virgin?'

CHAPTER NINE

'TECHNICALLY,' said Emma, 'I suppose I was.'

'What the hell are you talking about—*technically*?' Zak demanded as he stared at her flushed face. 'Either you're a virgin, or you're not.'

Trying not to recoil from the accusation blazing from his eyes, Emma felt her pleasure evaporate. Their love-making had been so *incredible*—like she'd never dared dream it could be. She wanted to just lie there and re-live it—second by glorious second—only now Zak was about to ruin it with some intrusive Q and A session. Uncomfortably, she wriggled. 'Do we have to talk about this now?'

'Damned right we do!' he exploded, because he felt as if she'd somehow *tricked* him. *Again*! As if she had revealed one secret when she'd told him the truth about Nat—only for him to discover that there was another one lurking, just below the surface. How many secrets did this woman have? he wondered furiously. 'When would you like us to discuss it? When you're hanging drapes with Cindy listening on the sidelines?'

'Of course not!'

'So start talking!'

'What is there to say?' she questioned tiredly. 'Except that my marriage was never properly consummated.'

'But Louis Patterson was known as a sex god!'

'He was also a heavy user of drugs and alcohol!' She met his eyes, the hurt and the pain spiralling up inside her and threatening to spill out in angry tears. But she swallowed them down, damned if she would come over as any more vulnerable than she already did. 'Can't you work it out for yourself, Zak—or do I have to spell it out for you?'

There was silence for a moment. 'He was impotent?'

Emma nodded, her throat thick with emotion—because even though at the time she'd pored over medical books, which had told her that such a side effect was normal for addicts, that hadn't stopped her from feeling a failure, had it? As if it was somehow all her fault. If she'd been stronger, she'd have been able to get him clean and sober. If she'd been more attractive, he would have been able to consummate their brief marriage. And Louis had only compounded those feelings of guilt—telling her that he'd never had problems with any woman before her.

'Yes,' she answered bluntly. 'He was.'

For a moment Zak didn't say anything, just shook his head. He felt like a man who'd just opened his early-morning shutters and seen the night-time sky outside. 'I just can't believe it,' he said.

'Is it such a crime to be a virgin then, Zak?'

'That's a naïve question and you know it.' He stared at her golden fingernails, which gleamed against the pristine white of the duvet. What a mass of contradictions she was, with her tumble of pale hair and her siren's body—yet beneath all that she'd been concealing an innocence which had shocked him profoundly.

'It wasn't an assumption I would ever have made about you,' he continued. 'And part of you must have realised that. But either you didn't think to tell me, or you decided deliberately *not* to tell me. And I would have liked to have known, Emma—to have been given some kind of choice in the matter about whether I wanted to take your virginity. Why me? And why now?'

Any trace of post-orgasmic euphoria had now completely vanished and Emma shivered, reaching for the rumpled duvet and pulling it around her. Maybe she *had* been wrong not to tell him—but hadn't one of the reasons been fear that he would have walked away? That some misplaced sense of 'honour' would have stopped him from making love to her? And hadn't she felt as if she'd die if he didn't?

'Why you? I'm sure you don't need me to tell you that. You're a very attractive and charismatic man, Zak, and I couldn't stop myself, if you must know,' she said in a low voice. 'How's that for honesty?'

He mulled this over in silence for a moment. 'And there's never been anyone else?'

She could hear the incredulity in his voice. 'Never.' Because hadn't her experience with Louis reinforced all her jaded views about men—views which had been formed by watching her mother operate? Louis had left her feeling inadequate and a failure and yet, in a way, it had been a *relief* to believe that she was frigid. To reassure herself that men were nothing but trouble and that she no longer had to venture down that particular road. Shunning the opposite sex hadn't been a problem at all—at least, not until the day she'd walked into Zak's office. And from that moment on, her feelings had given her nothing but trouble. 'I thought there might be something wrong with me. That maybe I was frigid.'

'Only now you've discovered that you most definitely aren't?' He gave a short laugh. 'I must say this is the first time in my life I've ever felt like a stud. Like I've been used to prove a point—and I'm not sure I like it very much.'

Emma realised that he'd added yet another accusation to the fast-growing list of complaints against her. And yet, why was he acting so hard done by? It wasn't as if it had been some long and slow candlelit seduction, was it? It had been fast and furious, almost *angry* sex—and surely for a man like Zak that must be something of a relief. It wasn't as though she was going to start reading too much into it—not when it had been motivated by anger and lust.

'Okay, it was a big mistake and we should never have done it,' she said, wriggling over to the side of the bed. 'So I'll get out of your hair and out of your bed and we can both try to forget it ever happened.'

The supple movement of her pale body made him harden. 'I don't want you to get out of my bed,' he said savagely. 'I don't want you going anywhere!'

'Don't feel you have to sugar-coat your disgust to try to spare my feelings!'

He leaned across and caught hold of her, and as the

duvet fell away to reveal the lush spill of her breasts he sucked in a deep breath. 'I'm not sugar-coating anything,' he said unevenly. 'And I can assure you that disgust is the very last thing on my mind right now.'

Hating herself for her compliance but unable to resist him when he looked at her like that, she allowed him to pull her into his arms. 'Really?'

'Really. I'm just a little dazed by my discovery and hoping that…' His words faded as he turned his lips and began to kiss the soft skin of her upper arm.

Fighting to prevent her eyelids from fluttering to a close, Emma stared at the tangled black gleam of his hair. 'Hoping that wh-what?'

He heard the waver of uncertainty in her voice and suddenly he felt anger for all she had endured. A mother who had been an appalling role model and who, it seemed, had pushed her into an unsuitable marriage when she was still heartbreakingly young. And then some thoughtless junkie of a husband who'd made her believe she was frigid. His voice softened. He didn't have to add to that list by being such a *brute*, did he? 'That you enjoyed what just happened, after what has been a very long wait.'

Now Emma was wide awake. Was that sympathy she heard in his voice—or was it the dreaded pity, which she'd always gone out of her way to avoid? Maybe he looked on her as some kind of freak because she happened to have reached the age of twenty-nine before losing her virginity. She looked at him suspiciously. 'Are you asking me to mark you out of ten?'

'No.' He laughed as he pulled her right back against him. 'I've never felt it necessary to request a scorecard.'

Probably because he'd get a gold star after every performance, she thought. She tried to hold on to what she felt was righteous indignation, but it wasn't easy. Not when he had drifted his lips to the curve of her jaw, an area she wouldn't have ever dreamt could be erogenous. But how wrong could she be? Because when Zak gave that tiny, barely there flick of his tongue, she was unable to stop the helpless tremble of her body. And suddenly she couldn't stop herself from wrapping her arms tightly around his neck and putting her face very close to his.

'Zak.'

'Shh.' He lifted his head so that his lips were soft against hers and he teased them open with his tongue. Shouldn't he delight her again—to reinforce that she was a deliciously healthy and normal young woman? Couldn't he give her the gift of physical enlightenment, even if he wasn't emotionally equipped to offer her any more than that? 'The second time can be even better.'

'B-better?'

'Mmm. Slower. More…'

'Zak!'

'Mmm?'

'What…what are you doing?'

He raised his head from its current location just south of her belly, his eyes gleaming in a way which made Emma's heart give a powerful kick. 'I'm about to lick you where every woman likes best to be licked and which might make conversation a little difficult. So you'll forgive me if I don't answer any more of your questions for a while.'

She wanted to protest that mentioning what other women liked wasn't the most diplomatic thing to say in the circumstances. She opened her mouth to tell him so but by then his dark head was buried between her thighs and his tongue was darting into her... Oh, God! He was actually kissing her...*there*—and the only sound she made was a gasp of disbelief that something could feel this good.

Softly, she moaned as his mouth worked some kind of sensual magic—her inhibitions melting away as she squirmed beneath the precision of his questing tongue. For a moment, she couldn't believe that this was really her—uptight Emma Geary writhing as her boss kissed her in the most intimate place imaginable and made her feel as if he was *feasting* on her.

Her second climax surprised her almost as much as the first—but then, she hadn't been expecting either. And she suddenly realised that sexual fulfilment didn't have to be something which hovered frustratingly just out of range. That if you were with the right man, it could happen as easily as breathing.

'Zak,' she whispered, wondering if it would be the wrong thing to do to fling her arms around his neck and to thank him. But he still didn't seem in the mood for any kind of conversation because he didn't even wait for the sweet spasms to subside before moving over her and thrusting deep inside her again.

Acutely aware of her own inexperience, she wondered if he was enjoying this as much as she was. But then the rhythm of his body changed and she felt him shudder. Heard the muffled exclamation he made in Greek and revelled in the way he kissed the top of her head afterwards, his hand snaking possessively around her waist, and he gave a deep sigh of contentment.

Silently, she clung to him—not wanting to break the warm spell which made it ridiculously easy for her to start wondering what this might be like on a full-time basis. Would it always be this amazing? Zak had been tender and considerate as a lover, even though she'd known he was angry at her deception. Just imagine what it might be like if he was in a *good* mood!

'Zak?' she questioned softly, when she realised from the sound of his steady breathing that he was fast asleep.

Slowly, she turned her head to look at his soft, parted lips and the starkness of his ebony hair against the snowy pillow. How completely relaxed he looked. His big body was sprawled out, all gleaming olive skin and honed muscle as he took up most of the bed. She thought he was the most beautiful thing she had ever seen and she could have lain there looking at him for hours. But even as she was revelling in the visual feast, dark thoughts began to eat away at her precarious self-esteem.

What had he said? *I'm about to lick you where every woman likes best to be licked.* Emma bit her lip and turned her gaze up to the ceiling. He had made her sound as if she was just the latest in a long line of lovers—and maybe that had been his intention.

Because that was *exactly* what she was. In fact, she probably only qualified for one-night-stand status.

She forced herself to confront the facts, no matter how painful they might be. His proud, Greek nature was appalled by her background, he'd told her that himself—and that much hadn't changed. Why, he'd even gone to the trouble of shipping her across the Atlantic so that he could separate her from his brother.

So what did she think was going to happen now that she'd had sex with him? That he'd take her to that very expensive jewellery shop situated on the eighth floor of his hotel and purchase one of those whopping great diamond rings which glittered so enticingly in the window? She winced. Not all men made ridiculously over-the-top gestures, the way Louis had done. And hadn't she learned the hard way that those gestures were empty ones? Zak had been fired up by lust and anger and they were no basis for anything solid, or lasting.

She had to get real. To look at the possibilities which lay open to her and then decide what to do. She thought about spending the night here, all wrapped up in his warm body, and temptation whispered over her skin. And then she imagined Zak waking up and thought about what they'd actually say to each other.

The most likely outcome was that he would open his eyes and regret everything that had happened last night. And wouldn't walking out of his suite wearing a crumpled evening dress in the harsh light of morning only add to her own feelings of remorse? Why, she didn't even have a toothbrush, let alone a hairbrush! Imagine if she bumped into that nice woman who made her bed each morning—or ran into Cindy. Emma flinched. If it was to be a one-off, then surely at least she could emerge with her pride intact. There'd be no need for any awkward farewells if she absented herself first.

Silently, she pushed aside the duvet and held her breath as she slipped from the bed. But, mercifully, Zak didn't stir and Emma quietly scooped up her underwear, shoes and dress and carried them into the sitting room. Her fingers were trembling as she dressed, terrified that he would wake up. And she couldn't bear the thought of facing him—afraid that he would look into her eyes and be able to read her thoughts. To realise that the whole experience had left her with more than the discovery that she was as normal as any other woman. And just as vulnerable. She felt bruised and raw—as if the protective skin she had grown around her heart had been stripped away. Nagging away at her was the growing fear that she could really start to *care* for Zak Constantinides.

Just before she opened the door, she caught sight of herself in the vast mirror which hung over the marble fireplace, freezing with horror as she saw the image reflected back at her. Her blond hair looked like the 'before' photo in a shampoo ad and her dress was so crumpled it could have been mistaken for a high-class duster. But it was her face which shocked her the most—all dark, smudged eyes and kiss-bruised lips.

She looked *wanton*. As if she'd been designed with no other purpose in life than to provide a man with pleasure. Unable to hold back her revulsion, Emma shuddered.

Because that was how her mother had liked to look— the way she'd lured in all those sleazy men. Hadn't

Emma seen her looking like that when she'd been getting her own breakfast cereal before school? And hadn't she vowed that she would never, *ever* get like that herself?

Her fingers were trembling as she picked up her discarded clutch bag and quietly let herself out of Zak's suite.

CHAPTER TEN

'If I didn't know better, I'd ask whether you *always* crept out of a man's bed without even bothering to say goodbye.'

A feeling of foreboding whispered over her as Emma looked up into the glitter of Zak's eyes. Was that anger she could read in them—or merely frustration that she'd been the one to make the decision by leaving his bed last night? That, for once, he had not been the one calling the shots.

Inside her thin gloves, her fingers were cold, and maybe the weather was too inclement to keep sitting outside and working on the terrace like this, but she'd felt closed in and *restless* after her night of passion with her Greek boss. She'd felt the need to escape—knowing that there was no real escape and that eventually he would come and find her.

'I didn't want to wake you,' she said weakly.

'Why not?'

'Because...' She hesitated for a moment before the words came spilling out—because what was the point of playing games? Hadn't she pretty much bared her soul after he'd made love to her last night? Didn't Zak Constantinides know more about her than any other person—her ex-husband and mother included? 'Because I thought that you might wake up this morning, regretting what had happened.'

For a moment there was silence and, like someone who couldn't resist scratching at a scab, Emma couldn't stop herself from probing further. 'Did you?'

Zak studied her pale face and furrowed brow. Her hair was piled up haphazardly on her head and, in her jeans and warm jacket, she couldn't have looked more different from the white silken goddess who'd danced in his arms last night. And maybe that had been her intention. He considered her question and the very fact she'd asked it spoke volumes about her lack of experience. A sophisticated woman wouldn't have dreamed of being so upfront, so early in an affair—of laying herself open to the possibility of rejection. But one thing he didn't do was dishonesty. He'd never given a woman hope where hope there was none.

He thought about the paparazzi who had captured their angry exit from the party and his mouth hardened. By now, every newsdesk in the western world would have it on their files. Its placement would depend on whether or not it was a light day for news—but inevitably it would be accompanied by the speculative splash about the 'mystery blonde' in his life. 'It probably wasn't the best idea in the world,' he said heavily.

Emma felt the sudden sinking of her heart. 'You didn't enjoy it?'

His mouth hardened. If it had been any other woman

than Emma asking him that particular question he would have told them not to be so damned disingenuous. But the anxiety in her eyes looked genuine and, given her particular history, wasn't it essential that he reassured her without filling her with false hope? 'I enjoyed it very much,' he said carefully. 'As, I think, you did?'

As if he needed to ask that! She wondered what it must be like to be Zak. To know that you were the most amazing lover and never have to suffer from any doubts or worry on that score. Did every woman he slept with feel the way he'd made her feel last night—as if she'd flown up to the sky and scooped up an armful of stars?

'Yes,' she whispered.

'Let's just hope that Nat doesn't see any paparazzi photos of us together.'

Her mouth flew open. 'But I told you—there was never anything between me and Nat.'

For a moment he said nothing. Didn't she understand the basic rivalry between brothers; between men themselves? No, of course she didn't—it was easy to forget how limited her experience was. 'I just think it's better if you say nothing—unless the subject arises.'

She tried not to flinch but it wasn't easy. Not when he was making her feel like a clump of dust which needed to be kicked underneath the carpet, out of sight.

'I wouldn't dream of saying anything. Don't worry, Zak—I won't breathe a word to a living soul. And I can leave right now if it's easier,' she added quietly. 'It'll be simple enough for me to leave instructions for Cindy— she's a bright girl and she knows what to do. Most of the stuff has been ordered—it's just a question of installing it within the next few days. The whole project can be wrapped up within the week and you won't actually need me for the opening.'

His eyes narrowed. 'Usually when I go to bed with a woman, it doesn't result in her wanting to put as much distance between us as possible,' he offered drily.

There was a pause. 'I didn't say I wanted to.' She stared down at her gloved hands as she drew in a deep breath, terrified he would see the vulnerability and the sheer *wanting* written all over her face. And wasn't it something of a shock to discover that deep down she was needier than she'd thought? Needier than she wanted to be. She found herself wanting to fling her arms around Zak's neck and cling to him—to pull his mouth to hers and have him kiss her again. And wouldn't that be a complete turn-off for a man like him? 'I just think it's probably for the best if I *did* go.'

Zak looked at the pale gleam of her blond head, thinking that maybe she was cleverer than he'd given her credit for. Maybe she was doing this untouchable thing this morning, knowing how tantalising he would find it. Because there was nothing that appealed to him more than something he thought he couldn't have. Was she clever enough to instinctively understand that?

'You're not going anywhere,' he said softly, seeing the startled expression in her pale eyes as she looked up at him. 'You're going to work today as usual, and then, at eight o'clock tonight, I'm taking you out for dinner.'

'Dinner?'

'Is that such an extravagant suggestion in the circumstances? You do need to eat dinner.' His eyes gleamed. 'Unless you have other plans.'

She pursed her lips against a smile which was threatening to split her face in two, because surely such overwhelming enthusiasm was completely uncool? 'Oh, I think I can manage dinner.'

'Good. I have meetings in another part of town, so I'll send a car to pick you up and meet you at the restaurant. How does that sound?'

'Sounds fine,' she answered as he stood up, and she waited in vain for him to kiss her, or squeeze her arm—or *something*. Some affectionate touch to indicate that last night she'd been gasping out her orgasm in his arms and that afterwards she'd had to bite back her trembling tears of gratitude. But he gave her nothing but a quick smile before walking out of the ballroom.

She realised that she still didn't know whether he regretted what had happened, but she also knew that analysis was dangerous—that it could drive you crazy if you let it. She put him out of her mind while she and Cindy deliberated over candles for the table settings and then spent almost an hour positioning a new painting on the wall until she was completely satisfied with it.

'You're such a perfectionist, Emma!' teased Cindy.

Emma smiled back. 'I call it attention to detail—the secret of success for an interior designer.'

But her nerves were back in force as she got ready for dinner—especially when she picked up the newspaper which had been shoved underneath the door of her hotel room. Flicking through it, she stilled when she reached the social pages and found a photo of her emerging from the party, with Zak.

It was a long time since she'd seen a photo of herself in a paper and she hated it as much now as she had done back then. The body language between them was telling. Zak looked dark-faced and *furious* while she hurried to keep up with him, looking like an anxious little mouse. She wondered if Nat *would* see the photo—and how he would interpret it.

Her mood now subdued, she chose a simple black dress worn with a long string of pearls. Pinning up her hair, she slipped on a warm jacket before going downstairs, where the doorman directed her to a waiting car.

A sense of unreality washed over her as she was driven across the city, and, when they drew up outside a nondescript building in the meat-packing area, she was sure the driver had the wrong address. Until Emma remembered that, in the world of the super-rich, less was definitely more. And that the pared-down and unexpected was currently considered far more chic than the overly ostentatious.

She gave Zak's name but was informed that he hadn't yet arrived and would she prefer to wait for him at the bar or go directly to their table?

She opted for the table. Her high-headed walk through the sumptuous room belied the nervous beating of her heart—her insecurities rising to taunt her. What was she doing here—agreeing to have dinner with a man who couldn't even be bothered to turn up on time? She ordered water and tried to sip it without feeling self-conscious but she was aware that she was the only single woman in the room and that realisation frayed at her already frayed nerves.

After a seemingly endless wait, Zak arrived with the discreet flurry which greeted him everywhere. She watched his progress towards her in his dark suit and pristine shirt, her heart beating unwillingly fast in response to that first sight of him. In the soft light his olive skin gleamed like gold and her body shivered in recognition of the fact that last night he had been hers. He pulled out the chair opposite hers. 'Sorry I'm late.'

'Don't worry about it,' she said. 'I've had a fantastic time sitting here, judging all their design ideas and comparing them to mine!'

He studied her, his heart giving a sudden hard beat. 'You look very beautiful tonight.'

'Oh, this? It's only—'

'To which you reply, "Thank you, Zak!"'

'Thank you, Zak,' she echoed softly.

'That's better.' He picked up a menu and handed it to her. 'They have a wide vegetarian selection here.'

She looked at him in surprise. 'You remembered.'

'I have a very good memory for detail,' he said, but his tone was thoughtful. She was surprised by small kindnesses, he acknowledged suddenly. She certainly wasn't as tough as he had initially thought, and maybe that meant he should play carefully with her. Maybe he shouldn't even have invited her out to a dinner which might make her believe that this relationship was going anywhere.

Yet wasn't last night's loss of her virginity and her subsequent enjoyment of sex supposed to herald the liberation she obviously needed? Couldn't this be the start of a whole new chapter for her? He'd shown her that sex could be good—and, after a little more instruction, she could go out into the world and start living her life all over.

'Did you...did you see the photo in the paper?' she questioned tentatively.

'I did.' His mouth flattened. 'I had them pull it from the online addition.'

'They let you do that?'

'They'd do pretty much anything for an exclusive interview. Don't worry about it—I'll do the best I can to make sure they leave you alone.'

His words sounded protective—as if nothing could ever touch her or hurt her if Zak was looking out for her. And yet even she, with her laughable lack of experience, knew that thinking that way was dangerous. Really dangerous. 'Thanks,' she said.

Zak allowed himself to relax as he studied her. Tonight her nails were scarlet, contrasting vividly against her little black dress, and he imagined them scraping delicately over his heated flesh.

Suddenly, he found himself wishing that he'd just ordered in room service—except he recognised that he owed her more than that. He had little in the way of a conscience but he knew he needed to tread carefully with Emma. If this ended when she took that plane back to England—as he suspected it would—he didn't want her feeling as if there had only been one thing on his mind. Even if it were true.

'So what's with the nails?' he murmured.

She put the menu down and blinked at him. 'The nails?'

He picked up her hand and caressed each scarlet-tipped finger. 'I've noticed that you always paint your nails different colours—which is a little at odds with the fact that you don't often wear make-up.'

Emma was surprised. He really *did* have a keen eye for detail. She looked down at her fingers, which were currently being dwarfed by his. 'Because my job is all about presentation, and when you're an interior designer, people always look at your hands—especially when you're showing them fabrics or pointing at a book. Jeans and T-shirts can easily be overlooked as part of a working uniform, but if your hands look unkempt—well, you'll be judged negatively.'

'I see. And is the subliminal message you're sending out tonight—that you're a scarlet woman?'

Emma swallowed, loving the sensation of his hand holding hers but also feeling a little daunted by the sensual look he was slanting at her across the table. Intimacy in the bedroom was one thing, but here—in the middle of some chic restaurant? How on earth was she supposed to react? She felt like a learner driver who'd just been told she was about to compete in a Grand Prix event. 'No,' she said quickly. 'It's just that red goes very well with black.'

'What a pity.' He let go of her hand as the waiter took their order and the sommelier offered them each a glass of champagne.

She wondered if she should have said that yes, she wanted to be a scarlet woman for the evening—was that what he expected of her? Were they supposed to be getting to know one another or were they supposed to be flirting? She thought about the way her mother used to act whenever any of her lovers were around. That way she'd had of fluttering her eyelashes and that stupid simpering thing she used to do. Well, Emma couldn't and wouldn't do that—and neither did she want to. What she wanted more than anything was to know what made Zak Constantinides tick—and surely their new intimacy meant that she could ask him stuff like that without coming over as intrusive?

'You know quite a lot about me,' she observed.

'You're angry that I hired a detective?'

She shrugged, because the truth was that she had almost forgotten about that. 'Maybe if I had your degree of power and influence, I might have done the same. What I was trying to say is that the balance of knowledge between us isn't very equal. You know stacks about me, while I don't know much about you.'

He raised his eyebrows. 'Only what Nat has told you, presumably.'

'He gave me the bare bones.'

'Such as?'

She picked up a heavy silver fork to toy with the Caesar salad which the waiter had placed before her. 'He told me about your privileged childhood.'

'Privileged?' He gave a short laugh. Was that how Nat had portrayed it? 'That's one way of describing it, I suppose. And did he tell you about the woman who came to work for my family as a nanny?'

She heard the raw anger which had entered his voice

and, cautiously, she nodded. 'He mentioned something about your parents' marriage ending and your father remarrying.'

Bitterly, Zak thought how easy it was for history to be precised into a few simple statements. How innocuous you could make the past sound if only you picked the right words. And it wasn't innocuous at all, was it? It was as dark and as twisted as all relationships.

'Did he tell you that the woman was much younger? All luscious curves and long blond hair.' There was a heartbeat of a pause. 'A bit like you.'

He saw her flinch and remembered the first time he'd seen her—thinking that he had been programmed to dislike women like her. And how wrong he had been. He'd been wrong about Emma in a lot of ways, he realised.

'No, he didn't tell me that.'

'She was barely twenty years old,' he continued, and he wondered if it was because he'd bottled up these words for so long that they now came spilling out. Or whether it had anything to do with the soft understanding in Emma Geary's green eyes. 'And my father was well into his fifties by then, so of course he was immensely flattered.'

For a moment, he faltered. 'Perhaps I wouldn't have blamed him for *sleeping* with her—I imagine that few men could have resisted the sight of that body wearing those tiny little bikinis around the pool. I know that my friends found plenty of reasons to come swimming that summer.'

He had been eaten up with shame and guilt that his

friends—all on the heady brink of adolescence—should have so blatantly desired the woman who had helped to break his mother's heart.

'What happened?' Emma whispered as she saw the ravaged look on his face.

He felt an acrid taste in his mouth. 'What happens rather frequently nowadays, but which was rarer back then—especially in the circles in which we moved. My father announced that he was in love, that he wanted a divorce and that he intended to marry the girl. My mother never got over it.' And now Zak realised that he was doing that thing himself. Of painting the past with a few brushstrokes which conveyed nothing but the barest facts. Because wasn't it disloyal to his mother's memory to recount the painful way she had crumbled? To recall how she'd wasted away, refusing to eat—as if that would bring back her errant husband.

It hadn't, of course. Her errant husband had been too busy indulging his new love to ever consider going back to the old one. He'd been too blown away by all that new sex to realise that his young bride was working her way through his fortune with an efficiency which might have been almost admirable, had it not been so destructive.

'The crazy thing was that nobody was happy,' he said slowly. 'My father slowly realised he'd made the biggest mistake of his life. That what he had experienced was lust, not love. He married a woman who spoke a different language—who was from an entirely different culture. Her values were not his values. I was estranged from him for years and could only watch helplessly from the sidelines as my mother's health deteriorated and his fortune was bled away by my…'

'Stepmother?' she prompted softly.

'No, not that!' His grey eyes blazing fire, his words were bitten out with ruthless precision. 'I would *never* call that woman mother—for she made a mockery of the word!'

'What…what happened?' asked Emma tentatively as she saw his face grow dark and stormy with memory.

He shrugged, as if it didn't matter. As if it had been nothing to him when, in fact, it had been everything. 'I cared for Nat during our mother's illness and after her death—and I cared for my father when that bitch left him without a penny to his name. And then, slowly, I built up the Constantinides fortune all over again.'

Emma was silent for a moment as much of his behaviour now became clear. How helpless he must have felt as he'd watched the deterioration of his previously safe world. The divorce, the death and then the loss of money and status. To a proud man like Zak, it must have been almost unendurable.

Yet didn't those events explain his need to control and to stamp his influence on everything around him? He had been left to care for his little brother and his protectiveness for Nat suddenly became understandable. And so too did his overwhelming drive to succeed. She'd thought that he had inherited the Constantinides fortune—she hadn't realised that he'd built it up from scratch.

She sat looking into the darkened pain of his grey eyes wondering why he'd opened up and told her all this, when his next words made it clear.

'Does that answer your question about why I've never settled down and married?'

There was a pause. 'I don't remember asking you that question, Zak.'

'No. But you were thinking it.' His grey eyes bored into her. 'If not now—then some time in the past.'

She thought how easy it would be to adopt an air of outrage—to accuse him of having an unspeakably large ego. But Emma thought about what he'd just told her and suddenly she found that she didn't want to retaliate, no matter what the provocation. He'd been hurt, she realised. Badly hurt. Couldn't she show him a little thoughtfulness without wanting anything in return? Couldn't she tell him the truth?

'Yes, I was,' she admitted. 'And I'm probably not the only woman to wonder why a man who seems to have it all—should be so unremittingly single.'

Zak was taken aback by her candour and even more surprised by another urge to elaborate. He picked up his glass and drank some claret. 'You talked about equality earlier—well, in my experience there is no true equality in relationships between the sexes. One person always loves too much and the other not enough.'

'Is that what happened with Leda?' she ventured boldly, remembering the woman with the short dark hair she'd seen in London. The woman who had persuaded

him to turn a room of his New York hotel over to weddings. Remembered, too, Nat's words to his brother…
that everyone had thought they would marry one day.

'Leda was the closest thing I ever got to what most
people settle for, yes,' he said roughly. 'But I liked
her too much to ever want to hurt her—and I couldn't
guarantee that I wouldn't do that.' He raised his glass
in silent toast. 'Anyway, she's marrying someone else
now—so it's all worked out for the best.'

Emma wondered if she was imagining the regret in
his voice—but she suspected he had told her as much
as he was going to. It had been a brutally honest assessment but she guessed it was also a warning to her. *Don't
get too close to me,* he seemed to be saying. *Because
nothing will ever come of it.*

'So now you know all about my past…does it shock
you?' His eyes lanced her a question and when she
didn't answer, he continued, 'Some people don't do
long-term relationships, Emma, and I'm one of those
people. It frustrates the hell out of women and they
spend a lot of time trying to change my mind—but they
never do. Which leaves me wondering whether you still
want to spend the night with me?'

It was, as they said, the sixty-four-thousand-dollar
question.

Emma met the pewter gleam of his eyes. He was
promising nothing—he couldn't have made that clearer
if he'd tried. But knowing that didn't change a thing
because the answer was that she didn't really have a
choice.

Hadn't she waited all her life for a man to make her

feel the way that Zak did? And even if it was doomed not to last—was she really willing to turn her back on it now that she'd found it?

'Actually, I do,' she said, in as light a tone as possible. 'And this time I'll stay all night.'

CHAPTER ELEVEN

FOR the first time in her life, Emma felt like somebody's girlfriend. Like one of those women for whom life was 'normal.' Just an ordinary woman who was seeing a man, while deciding how much they liked each other. And she'd never had that before.

With Louis, everything had been so hush-hush and hidden away. His management had worried that another marriage might dent his latest reinvention as rock's sexy bad boy and, consequently, she'd been kept out of view as much as possible—at least until the wedding had taken place. Then she'd been brought out at every opportunity—her youth a testimony to her husband's supposed virility. But she'd only ever had a fraction of her husband's attention. The women who eagerly pressed their phone numbers into his hand were often greeted with a smile rather than a rejection.

With Zak it was different. She'd thought he might tire of her after one or two dates. Or that he'd try to see her as little as possible—and then mainly for sex. But he had surprised her. His chivalry, she'd realised, had not been a one-off.

He'd taken her to some amazing restaurants and galleries and once to a concert at Carnegie Hall. He'd managed to get tickets for Broadway's hottest show and she had found herself laughing at the corniest musical she had ever seen until tears had run down her cheeks. And then she'd looked up to find Zak watching her, shaking his head in slight bemusement as he'd pulled a perfectly laundered white handkerchief from his pocket and solemnly handed it to her.

There'd been no sense of him hiding her away. And just because he'd introduced her as his interior designer, on secondment from his London hotel—well, she wasn't really in a position to be disappointed by his not-quite-accurate assessment of their relationship, was she? If sometimes she felt as if she were holding a handful of sand which was slowly slipping through her fingers—well, there wasn't a lot she could do about it. Emma knew that none of this was supposed to last—she was just trying to enjoy it while it did.

But the clock was inexorably ticking away and she felt as Cinderella must have done as the hands edged towards midnight. The opening of the wedding room was scheduled for the end of the week and her ticket home was booked. She would be flying out of JFK and leaving Zak behind. And she didn't dare confront what that might feel like.

On the night before the opening, he took her to a fabulous skyscraper restaurant, where outside the sky was like a black velvet canopy, filled with stars. A fingernail moon gleamed through the windows and the dazzle of crystal and flicker of candles all contributed to a heady overload of her senses.

'I ought to be working,' she said weakly as she ran her finger around the edge of her champagne glass.

'You've been working all day.'

'I know. But it's—'

'It's going to be perfect. Of that, I have no doubt, *chrisi mou.*'

Her hand not quite steady, Emma put her glass down because she couldn't help thrilling when he spoke to her in Greek. Usually, it was something profound or muffled at the height of his orgasm—but he never usually used endearments in the public arena of a restaurant. 'What does that mean?'

'It means my "golden one".'

'That's…nice.'

'Mmm.' He heard the unmistakable note of hope in her voice and knew that she wanted more, because that was what women were programmed to want. But he could not give her more—other than the very obvious. His hooded eyes flicked to her plate. 'You're not eating very much.'

'Neither are you.'

'Maybe that's because I'm wondering why we're spending our last night here, when we could be doing something much more enjoyable back at the hotel.'

'But you've just ordered a bottle of champagne which cost as much as I take home in a week.'

'Who cares about that?' he questioned roughly. 'Let's get the check.'

They left the restaurant and kissed like a couple of

teenagers in the back of a cab—hailed because he'd told his driver to return at eleven. Emma felt an unstoppable sense of suppressed excitement until the moment when they were alone in his suite and she began to tug impatiently at his jacket.

'Shouldn't I have taught you a little more finesse?' He laughed as he shrugged it from his shoulders and dextrously tossed it onto one of the sofas.

'Is it finesse you want?' she breathed, her fingers moving to the buckle of his belt and sliding down his aroused length.

'God, no. No. Just keep doing what you're doing.'

It was fast and it was passionate—and afterwards they went to bed and did it again. And again. So that by the time Emma stirred, it was against a heavy tide of sleepiness and the sense that the space on the bed beside her was empty. In the murky dimness of the morning light, she could just make out Zak's tall silhouette moving quietly around the suite. 'What time is it?'

'Ten after six.'

She stifled a yawn. 'That's early.'

'Mmm.'

'You've got meetings?' she questioned as she leaned over to switch on the bedside lamp.

Zak watched as the soft apricot light transformed her pale and curvy body into that of a golden goddess. How could she look so damned good in the morning? he wondered. And how come she always felt so good in the night, too? *And tonight would be the very last night, he realised. Tomorrow she would fly back to England and the distance between them would inevitably rup-*

ture their relationship. 'I'm afraid I do,' he murmured. 'Wall-to-wall meetings all day long.'

'Oh.'

'There's no point pouting, Emma.'

'Was I pouting?'

'Yes, you were.' He walked towards the bed and bent down to drop a kiss on her sleep-ruffled hair, inhaling the scent of roses and shampoo. 'Being provocative without even realising it. Anyway, you have far too much to do than to mess around in bed with me. Tonight's your big night, isn't it?'

Emma's smile didn't slip. Yes, tonight was her big night—the opening of the wedding room, with all the accompanying fanfare. For her, it was the moment of job completion and, hopefully, one of triumph, too. Her work would be laid bare for others to judge and how it was seen tonight would largely determine its popularity.

Caterers and florists would be arriving throughout the day and later the room would be put on show to New York's finest. There would be prospective clients and party animals, as well as journalists who would be recording the event and garnering publicity for Zak's latest venture.

And afterwards? When the dried-up canapés and half-drunk glasses of champagne had been cleared away—what then? She bit her lip, unable to stop the sudden sinking of her heart. Her work would be completed. She would be free to go back to London…leaving Zak behind.

She tried to shake off her feeling of impatience—as much at her own stupidity as anything else. Because she'd *realised* the danger of becoming the lover of Zak Constantinides all along. She had realised it and chosen to ignore it, with an arrogance fuelled by her own passionate desire. Forgetting that if you flew too close to the sun, you tended to get burned, when she, of all people, should have known that.

'It certainly is,' she said brightly. 'The biggest night of all.'

His lips moved to her bare shoulders. 'So you don't want me wearing you out with sex beforehand, now, do you?'

She couldn't help herself. Her hands reached up to his neck, her fingers caressing the thick waves of hair which grew there. 'Don't I?' she whispered, her mouth brushing against the newly shaved smoothness of his jaw. 'Are you quite sure about that?'

It was the most innocent of touches and yet Zak felt the jackknifing of desire shafting through him, his hand automatically slipping down to cup the heavy weight of her breast. How in tune their bodies were, he thought. He'd never known such instant compatibility—not from women with years more experience than Emma. Was that because he'd taught her pretty much everything she knew, or because he'd opened up to her with uncharacteristic frankness? Sometimes he felt as if she'd stripped away the protective layers with which he shielded himself—and glimpsed the person he kept hidden from the world. He felt as if Emma knew him better than anyone else—and didn't that scare him a little?

And now she was looking at him with those shining green eyes, her lips soft with promise and her body even softer as her thighs parted instinctively beneath the white swathing of the linen sheet.

For a moment he wavered—tempted to strip off his carefully pressed suit and drop it to the ground. To pull back the covers and lose himself in her molten sweetness. Briefly, he closed his eyes as he imagined that first delicious thrust before reminding himself that he didn't have time. More importantly, he didn't have the inclination to demonstrate just how persuasive he found her. Because wasn't it high time to build some immunity against her seductive hold on him—to prepare them both for her imminent departure?

Abruptly, he stepped away from the bed, raking his fingers back through his hair. *She was leaving tomorrow—and he had better get used to that.*

'Quite sure,' he growled. 'Just as I don't think it's a great idea having breakfast with the CEO of a major bank if I can still taste you on my lips and on my fingers. You need to be fresh and rested before you face a very critical New York audience. So go back to sleep and I'll see you later at the opening. Okay?'

'Okay.' Filled with frustration and a sudden wariness about something she'd seen in his eyes, Emma lay back until the door had clicked shut behind him, but she was never going to get back to sleep after that. Instead, she showered and dressed and then painted her fingernails in a pearly white colour to reflect the wedding theme of the party. But despite the soothing strokes of the brush, her thoughts kept spinning off on to random tracks which always brought her back to the same place. Or, rather, the same person.

Zak.

She knew it was time to leave. She'd known that all along—and yet with each second that passed she re-alised how much it was going to hurt to say goodbye to him. Especially since now she had a catalogue of memories which felt stupidly and temptingly…*happy*.

Hadn't she prayed that Zak hadn't really meant it when he'd told her about his views on permanence? That he'd make an exception for her. Was she *mad*? Just because they'd shared a few soft and tender moments after orgasm and could make each other laugh, didn't mean it was any way permanent.

She was doing what she had vowed not to. Trying to cling to something which had a natural end in sight, just as her mother had always done when she'd sensed that one of her lovers was cooling towards her. And she had to stop it. Right now. She had to stop acting as if this were some great love affair and instead just enjoy showcasing a project on which she'd worked so hard.

Fired up by professional pride and a new determina-tion, she spent the rest of the day finalising last-minute details with Cindy. With barely a break for lunch, they worked straight through until five—giving themselves just under an hour to get ready before meeting down-stairs in the ballroom. Emma was wearing the dry-cleaned white dress she'd worn to Sofia's party—and Cindy was resplendent in a sapphire-blue playsuit, which echoed her eyes.

For a moment they gazed around the completed room in silence until Cindy spoke at last in a dreamy voice.

'Oh, Emma—it looks fantastic! Like…like something out of a *fairy tale*.'

Emma nodded, buoyed up by her young assistant's enthusiasm. 'It does, doesn't it?' she questioned. 'I think any woman would want to get married here.'

Pale, buttery drapes framed the enormous windows and contemporary mirrors reflected back even more light. Tables were laid with settings of silver and crystal and fragrant, creamy candles. And dominating a far corner of the room stood a beautiful statue of Aphrodite, which added just the right quirky finish. Emma had found it by chance in a little antique shop on 60th St and she liked the fact that the Greek goddess of love should be represented in a room designed to celebrate weddings.

The irony of her choice didn't escape her, either. A Greek goddess erected in silent tribute to her own Greek god who was so damning about the concept of love. What had he said? *That one person always loves too much and the other not enough…*

Forcing the memory from her mind, she looked around the room. 'Right, I'm just going to tweak the flowers.'

'And I'll go and have a last-minute chat with the head of security,' said Cindy, with a grin. 'Tickets are like gold dust and I want to make sure that nobody gets in who isn't supposed to.'

'I can't imagine that security would ever be a problem at the Pembroke.'

'No. But you never know.'

Once Cindy had gone, Emma busied herself with

last-minute touches, wondering if Leda would be the first bride to marry here—and wondering whether Zak would feel any pang of regret for the woman he'd come pretty close to marrying himself. Just before seven, the first guests started to arrive and, soon after that, her Greek lover appeared.

As soon as he walked into the ballroom, people began to cluster around him, like ants swarming on a spoonful of fallen jam—but he quickly detached himself and walked over to where she was standing, drinking a glass of mineral water.

For a moment he didn't speak, just gazed at her from between narrowed eyes, as if he was preserving her image for posterity. 'You must be very pleased,' he said softly.

Emma gave a wry smile. Did he have no inkling that inside her heart was breaking—knowing that tomorrow she'd be on that air-bus over the Atlantic, jetting out of his life for good?

'Very pleased,' she answered coolly. 'I don't imagine you'll have much trouble filling it with prospective brides and grooms. Oh…' Emma's voice momentarily trailed off as she saw a woman entering the ballroom—her dramatic black hair and eye-catching scarlet opera coat commanding instant attention from the other guests. 'Isn't that Leda?'

Zak turned his head to see the tiny brunette making her way towards them. 'So it is.'

'Zakharias!' The brunette embraced him in a flurry of smiles and scarlet silk. 'This is more beautiful than I ever dared wish for! A triumph!'

'Then it is Emma Geary you must thank, for it is all her work.'

Leda's dark eyes were turned towards Emma and a faint frown of recognition appeared on her brow. 'Ah, yes—I thought I recognised you. You're the woman who was in the restaurant that night in London, with Nat, aren't you? How *is* Nat?'

Emma felt a telltale flush of something which felt like guilt wash over her skin. What would Leda say if she knew the truth—that she had spurned Nat's advances, only to jump straight into bed with Zak? Would she think that she had betrayed and compromised both brothers by her actions? 'He was fine last time I heard from him,' she said truthfully. 'Though that was ages ago.'

'He's probably busy with work,' said Zak, his eyes pewter cool as they met hers. 'And speaking of work, will you excuse me? I think the mayor's just arriving.'

Emma could have *killed* him as he walked away, leaving her alone with his ex-girlfriend and a very uncomfortable feeling. He had cleverly made her sound like nothing but an employee to his ex and she wondered why she should find that so hurtful when it was nothing but the truth.

'Have you known Zakharias for very long?' Leda was asking.

Emma shrugged as she reluctantly dragged her gaze away from his progress through the admiring hordes of women. 'Only a matter of months—although it feels like years!'

'Yes. He does tend to have that effect on people.'

'Especially women,' said Emma, the words out of her mouth before she could stop them.

'Indeed.' Leda shot her a shrewd look before lowering her voice. 'And are you in love with him by any chance?'

Slowly, Emma met the other woman's dark eyes. 'That's a very personal question,' she said in a low voice.

'I know it is. I ask only because I was once in love with him myself. Me and the rest of the world, probably—though I think I got closer to getting him to commit than anyone else has ever managed.' She gave a short laugh. 'I honestly thought my world would end when he walked out of my life, but it didn't. I survived and met Scott and now we're going to be married and I couldn't be happier. Truly.' Her features softened. 'That's what I wanted to tell you, Emma. That there *is* life after Zakharias Constantinides.'

A waiter bearing canapés interrupted their talk but Emma felt that eating would have choked her—and by the time the waiter had left, Leda had drifted away to talk to someone else.

Emma's hands curled into two small fists, her thoughts in turmoil as all her forbidden fantasies crumbled to dust around her. Leda had told her nothing that Zak hadn't already made clear—but she had told her in that woman-to-woman way, which made it impossible to ignore. She felt like a child whose playmate had just informed them there was no such thing as Santa. She didn't *want* to spend her last night in New York facing up to the unpalatable truth! She didn't *want* to be told that there was life after Zak when all she wanted was to spend her life *with* him. She'd wanted to hold on to her hopeless dream for one last night...

'Why so melancholy, *chrisi mou*?' Zak's voice shattered her reverie and she looked up to see his glittering grey eyes fixed on her in question.

'Was I? I didn't mean to be,' she answered brightly.

His eyes narrowed. 'What did Leda say?'

'Nothing I didn't already know,' responded Emma.

'Oh?'

'Just that, although you were obviously a very hard act to follow, that she really *did* find happiness with someone else.'

'Did you tell her we were lovers?'

'No, Zak. I told you that I wouldn't breathe a word to anyone and I haven't. She probably guessed—I'd imagine that ex-lovers are probably very perceptive when it comes to such matters.'

'Emma—'

'But she seems to approve of the room,' she rushed on, cutting through an interjection she had no desire to hear. 'So at least I can leave New York with the satisfaction of knowing it's a job well done.'

Zak noticed the sudden acute pallor of her face and for the first time it occurred to him that he could have asked her to delay her departure for a day or two. Couldn't he have taken her away for a long weekend and said goodbye to her in some sort of style, rather than allowing this somewhat rushed farewell to happen?

The sound of chatter was swelling and the flow of laughter was indication enough that the party was a success—but suddenly he was filled with a sense of something unfinished. Without thinking, he brushed his fingertip along her bare forearm and saw her eyes darken at just that brief touch. And something in her instantaneous reaction awoke in him an answering need, which thundered through his blood like a fever. How did she do it? How the *hell* did she drive all sane thoughts clean out of his mind so that all he could think about was possessing her as urgently and as thoroughly as possible?

Swallowing down the suddenly unbearable desire which was making his body tense, he looked at her—resenting her golden-haired magnetism and her power over him even as he revelled in its inevitable outcome.

'Can I have a private word with you?' he questioned softly.

'Sure. When?'

'How about now?'

'But the party—'

'Needs neither of us. And I need to talk to you, Emma.'

'Need' was a word which Zak didn't do very often and Emma's heart was racing as they made their way out of the ballroom. Some stupid little spark of hope kept flaring up inside her—though it wavered momentarily as she realised that he was taking her to his empty office on the first floor.

'Zak?' she questioned uncertainly as the door slammed shut behind them and he pulled her into his arms. And the little flare of hope grew into a great big flame as she saw the intense look in his eyes. Had he brought her here because it was nearer? Because he couldn't wait a second longer to be alone with her? Was he maybe regretting her departure as much as she was?

'Emma,' he said as he looked down at her for one long, hard moment before lowering his mouth to hers.

Her lips opened beneath his as he kissed her with a passion she was used to—but there was something else in it, too. Something which underpinned it and felt almost like...*anger*? And that something seemed to ignite an answering flame in her. Suddenly she was on *fire* for him. Her fingernails scrabbled hungrily at his chest as he pulled the pins from her hair, allowing it to spill over her shoulders before levering her up against his aroused body.

'I want you,' he ground out, his hand sliding beneath her dress and working its way up her thigh to the cool silk of her thigh. 'Damn you, Emma Geary, but I want you. You're like a fever in my blood—do you know that?'

'Zak,' she breathed, his name leaving her lips with soft urgency. 'Oh, Zak. I want you, too. Always. *Always.*'

The stressed word was like a bucket of ice-water thrown all over him and suddenly he released her, seeming to steady his breath with difficulty as he walked over to the huge windows so that he was silhouetted against them like a towering black statue.

Emma's heart lurched as she looked across the room at the inexplicably dark expression on his face. What on earth was the matter with him? What had she said that was so wrong?

'What is it?' she whispered as she met the daunting glitter in his eyes.

For a moment Zak didn't answer as he fought against his unbearable desire. He wanted her so much. He wanted her so much he couldn't think straight. He'd wanted her even when he'd thought she was his own brother's lover!

A cold wave of guilt washed over him and so did the memory of that word. *Always.* Was Emma so certain of her hold over him that she thought she'd succeeded where so many others had failed? That she'd got her hooks into him for life? She was no different from any other woman and this was nothing but a powerful lust which would soon fade. Just the way all the others had faded...

'Take off your panties,' he said suddenly.

Something in the way he said it made Emma's blood run cold. *'What?'*

'You heard. Take your panties off.'

'Why?' she whispered.

His eyes met hers in a sizzling look which only yesterday might have had her melting. 'Oh, come on, Emma—you were an innocent who has become the most alluring of lovers, the most avid student of sex I've ever known.' His voice dipped. 'And I want you to strip for me in my office. It's a fantasy I've been nurturing for a while now. The memory of it will sustain me while I'm dealing with boring business calls. Instead of gazing out at skyscrapers, I can close my eyes and picture the magnificence of your soft thighs.'

Still she said nothing and, arrogantly, he let his hand

slide along the straining ridge at his fly, seeing the instinctive parting of her lips as he did so. 'So why the hesitation? You don't usually hesitate over my suggestions.'

'*Suggestion?*' she repeated, her breath coming very hot and fast in her rapidly drying throat as the reality of the situation came slamming home to her. And suddenly she realised that he was treating her the way that men used to treat her mother—like some sort of cheap *hooker.* 'Is that what you call it? You bring me up here while the party's still going on. And, for what? You want a striptease, no doubt followed by a quick bonk—'

'"A quick bonk"?' he echoed disbelievingly. 'I don't do *quick bonks*!'

'Whatever!' she flared back. 'The terminology isn't the point! What do you suppose all those guests at the party would think if I suddenly reappeared downstairs looking thoroughly ravished?'

'It isn't the role of my guests to have opinions about my private life,' he snapped.

'Except it isn't very *private*, is it, Zak? You bring me here and make me feel like a cheap tart—was that your intention?'

'You've stripped for me before.'

'That was in the bedroom!'

'We've only been lovers for a few weeks—surely that's a little early for conventionality to rear its head?' His mouth gave a wry twist. 'But if you're insisting on the proximity of a bed then we can go upstairs to my suite right now and do it there.'

To Emma's fury, she could feel the prick of tears at

her eyes. 'Why are you behaving like this, Zak?' she whispered.

He stared at her, her question striking at a conscience he had no desire to feel. Why indeed? Because it felt safer to push her away than to acknowledge the way she was making him feel inside? Because she needed to know where she stood? More importantly, *so did he*.

'Because I can,' he answered simply and gave a shrug as he saw the sudden tremble of her lips. 'I'm sorry.'

Emma stared at him, his words wiping away all the pretence she had allowed to fester and grow. All those stupid hopes and dreams that Zak might one day care.

Now she was forced to confront the truth—as she had been forced to confront it many times before. But this time she wasn't a helpless child who was dependent on an erratic mother. And neither was she an inexperienced young woman who'd been blinded by a man's fame and her mother's ambition for her to make a 'good' marriage.

Now she was Emma. Grown-up Emma who wouldn't do what she knew to be the wrong thing. And the wrong thing would be to entertain any hope of a future with Zak. She'd known that right from the beginning—but she had been too blown away by her sexual awakening to listen to her very real doubts.

But she couldn't let the desires of her body influence her into making another dumb mistake with a man. And she couldn't let her foolish belief that she had fallen in love with him sway her either. She had to be strong. That didn't mean she had to be bitter. Just strong. To accept Zak for the man he was, not the man she wanted him to be.

'You don't have to be sorry,' she said quietly. 'You haven't done anything wrong.'

'I haven't?' he questioned, his eyes narrowing because he had expected a whole heap of accusations to come piling down on top of him.

'Not really. You're just being yourself.'

'Now why does that make me feel some kind of heel?'

'That wasn't my intention, I can assure you.'

And he nodded in comprehension, because he knew that. Emma didn't play mind games. In fact, she didn't do the stuff which women usually did. She didn't angle to have him buy her expensive gifts or to fill up his diary for the next year. All she'd ever done since that first time he'd taken her to his bed had been to become his perfect lover—except for now, when he had pushed her further than she had been willing to be pushed.

Yet wasn't it ironic that her refusal to play the role he had wanted her to play was making him *respect* her—so that instead of the frustration he should have been feeling, he now felt an overwhelming need to appease her?

'Look, just forget I ever asked,' he said easily. 'We'll go back down to the party and, after it's over, I'll take you for dinner here in the hotel—how does that sound?'

Ten minutes ago it would have sounded like heaven on earth, but not any more. Now it sounded exactly what it was—a sweetener for her anger and no doubt a way of ensuring that she would perform to his satisfaction in the bedroom, later.

'Tempting, but I'll pass.'

His eyes narrowed. 'You'll *pass*?'

It was the incredulity in his voice that did it. If ever Emma had needed proof that he was an arrogant and egotistical man who would never change, then now she had it.

'Yes, Zak, incredible as it may seem to you, I'll pass. My job here is done and I'm going to go up to my suite to pack because I'm leaving tomorrow. So I'll let you go back down to your guests and to entertain them. Who knows? You probably won't have any trouble finding a replacement stripper for the night!'

'Now you're making *me* sound cheap,' he grated.

'At least you know how it feels.'

For a moment they stood facing each other across the expanse of the minimalist office, their gazes clashing in a silent duel of wills.

'Let's be clear about one thing, Emma,' said Zak, breaking the silence at last when it became clear that she was not going to back down and change her mind. 'If this…*withdrawal*…of yours is supposed to make me your instant slave, then I have to tell you that it's the wrong tack to take. You see, I don't do emotional blackmail. I never have.'

Emma's mouth opened and then closed again, because she was afraid that she might do something as undignified as screaming aloud with frustration and rage. Or throwing a pot of pens at his smug face, just as she'd wanted to do that very first time when he'd summoned her in to see him.

'I feel sorry for you, Zak,' she said, in a shaking voice.

'There's so much good in the world, but you just never see it, do you? Because you're an emotional *coward*! Everywhere you look, you find some game or plot—some conniving woman determined to drag you up the aisle or to get you to commit. Well, I am not that woman—and I never will be. I wouldn't dream of wanting something from a man which wasn't given freely. I may not have much experience but that is something I *have* learnt! So you'll forgive me if I say goodbye and leave you now. I'm out of here first thing tomorrow—and, to be honest, I can't wait.'

She saw the disbelief which clouded the grey blaze of his eyes—and she saw something else, too. Something which looked like pain and was probably to do with the wounding of his wretched ego. Quickly, she turned away—before she revealed her own far more damning tears, grateful that her mother's dancing tuition meant she never had any problem keeping her back straight. At least she was leaving Zak with her head held high, even if inside her heart felt as if it were breaking.

CHAPTER TWELVE

As soon as she'd left Zak's office, Emma went to her suite and packed up her clothes before checking out of the Pembroke. It was pride which motivated her, but fear, too. Fear that Zak might come up and find her and use all that potent sex appeal to persuade her into changing her mind. And it would be wrong to fall into bed with him when he had the ability to make her feel like some sort of *hooker*. Now that the inequalities in their relationship had been revealed, she needed to put as much distance between them as possible before she got on that plane tomorrow.

Clutching her suitcase, she hurried out of the building and hailed a cab, which took her to another hotel, close to JFK. It was a mere 1.7 miles away from the airport and ran a free shuttle service. It was cheap and it was basic and it was exactly what she needed as a kind of antidote to the luxury of Zak's Pembroke. She found a strange kind of comfort in the bland magnolia walls and the highly glossed blue satin bedcover, which was stretched tightly over the high bed. She sat in the red-walled cafeteria and drank weak coffee at a formica table and the most stupid thing was that she felt *nostalgic*, because this was bottom end of the market. A place for people on a budget. She'd once lived on a budget before circumstances had catapulted her into a world where money ruled.

Yet money really didn't bring you happiness, did it? Look at Louis, squandering most of his vast fortune on drink and drugs. And look at Zak—who, for all his hotels and massive fortune, didn't seem to possess any kind of inner peace.

But she didn't want to think about Zak—with his stormy grey eyes and that way he had of kissing her, and holding her which made her feel as if she'd fallen into some kind of secret paradise. She wanted to forget that she'd lost her heart to a man she'd known from the outset had been dangerous.

He rang that night, as she sat on the blue-glossed bedspread, comfort-eating a doughnut and watching some horrendous game show on the giant TV screen. She saw the name 'Zak' flashing on the screen of her cellphone and she despaired as her heart gave a lurch. She wanted to pick it up. She wanted him to say the kind of things to her that she knew he was never going to say. Instead, she licked her sugary fingers and turned up the TV—so that the loud studio laughter blocked out the ringtone. And after that she switched the phone to silent and turned it face down on the table where she couldn't see it flashing.

He rang again as she sat waiting in the departure lounge at the airport, but still she didn't pick up. And when the delayed plane landed at Heathrow, she saw that he'd rung twice more. She was *not* going to speak to him—because what would be the point when everything had already been said? And surely hearing the silken lilt of his Greek accent would be counterproductive if it only increased this terrible aching in her heart. Glancing down, she saw that he'd left a voicemail message and she gave her first grim smile of the day as she pressed the delete button.

Back in London, she found the city suffering from some of the most unforgiving weather it had seen in years. The trees were stripped bare and the wind howled like a demented banshee. It felt as if nature were playing a cruel trick—making the elements reflect the miserable way she felt inside—and Emma shivered as she stared out at the dark sky.

Yet didn't she only have herself to blame? Knowing that she had thrown all her principles out of the window to sleep with a man like Zak?

Maybe... She bit her lip, plagued by the thought which kept buzzing around her head. Maybe she had been more influenced by the whiff of money and power than she'd previously admitted. So did that make her a hypocrite as well as a fool?

She was dreading returning to work at the Granchester—although she'd half expected to find a termination contract waiting for her on her return. And wouldn't that have been easier? To just close the curtains on this particular chunk of her life, and never need to peep behind them again.

But there was no such dismissal letter, and when she rang in to speak to Xenon—Zak's aide—it was to be told that there was a whole stack of work ready and waiting for her. Emma knew she should have been glad for the distraction, but instead her heart sank. She didn't want stuff *waiting* for her when all she felt like doing was closing the door of her apartment and staying there until this hurt had gone away.

In her silent bedroom, she unpacked—realising that it had been ages since she'd done anything as normal as going to the supermarket. She sent Nat a text, telling him she was back and saying that maybe they could meet for a drink some time. And the reply which came pinging back an hour later said, *Love to. Am away. Back next week. Em, think I'm in love!*

Emma wondered if this time he had found the real thing as she stared in the mirror, realising that she looked different—and not just because of her strained face. She *felt* different. Something had changed and she recognised that for the first time. *She* had changed. She had found the strength to walk away from something she knew to be damaging, even though it had hurt like hell to do so. Maybe inner strength was the consolation prize—the one good thing to emerge from the ashes of her dead relationship.

But she also realised that there was no going back. That she *had* used her friendship with Nat as a buffer against the rest of the world. And even if this love affair of his went the way of all the others, she couldn't just slip back into her old role. She couldn't keep reaching for that particular safety net, not if she wanted to live her life as fully as possible. She might not have Zak. She might not end up with anyone—but she just *might*. And didn't Leda's kind words spur her on to think that there might be some kind of happy future, even if it wasn't with the Greek lover she had grown to love, despite her determination not to?

The following morning, she went straight to Xenon's office where Zak's oldest aide greeted her with a crinkly smile as he leaned back in his chair. 'I hear you did good,' he said, waving her towards a vacant seat.

Emma sank into the chair and looked at him with wary eyes. 'You did?'

'Sure. The wedding room at the Pembroke is a massive success—they're already booked out until next May. Can you believe that?'

'That's fabulous,' said Emma, hating herself for her inability to resist asking, 'How…how did you hear?'

'You mean apart from the glowing reviews in the press and the fact that *Vogue* wants to shoot a wedding issue there?' Xenon beamed at her. 'It was Zak, actually. Not like him to take an interest in such minutiae—but he seems to be delighted. Unusually so. In fact, there's talk about you doing something similar, here.'

Emma stared at him. *'Here?'*

'Sure. Why not?' Xenon rubbed his fingers and thumb together as he mimed the international sign for making money. 'Lots of weddings in London—so why not capitalise on a fertile market?'

But Xenon's words shocked her into realising that she really couldn't go back. Or at least, not to the Granchester. How *could* she carry on working here when every wall and stick of furniture—every sheet of letterheaded paper—would remind her of Zak? Did she really think she could continue doing the same thing—

working on another wedding room—with any degree of enthusiasm, when just the thought of weddings made her want to bawl her heart out?

She shook her head. 'I can't do it, Xenon,' she gulped.

'What do you mean, you can't? Zak said you went down a storm in New York.'

'Maybe I did, but I still can't do it. In fact, I can't work here any more. I want…' She drew a deep breath as if giving herself time to comprehend the irrevocability of her next words. But the short pause which followed did nothing to change her mind. 'I want to hand my notice in.'

His eyes narrowed. 'Emma, are you *crazy*? Everything is just opening up for you.'

And everything was in danger of shutting down at the same time—her heart and her spirit and her hopes—if she allowed it to. This place was now steeped in bittersweet memories and she needed to be able to break away from the past and start a new life for herself. Again, she shook her head. 'I can't, Xenon. I have to go. There'll be a million brilliant people who'd love to take my place—so you've no worries on that score. Perhaps you could…well, perhaps you could let Zak know?' she questioned hoarsely.

Xenon's eyes narrowed. 'I think you'd better tell him yourself.'

The weight of the inevitable sat heavily on her shoulders and Emma's instinct was to turn on her heel and run. But surely she had the guts to tell him herself, after everything that had happened between them. 'Okay,' she said slowly. 'I'll ring him in New York tonight.'

'No need.' Xenon leaned forward to buzz his secretary and spoke into the intercom. 'Tell Zak that I have Emma in my office, will you?'

Emma sprang to her feet, aware of a sudden rage of emotions, which were making her heart pound so loudly that it felt as if it were about to leap from her chest. 'He's *here*?'

'Right here,' said Zak, walking straight into the office and making Emma wish that she'd stayed sitting because suddenly her legs had turned to jelly. Had she forgotten the impact of his presence—the charismatic lure of his jet-dark hair and olive skin? The way that he could look like some sort of Greek god in nothing but a pair of dark trousers and a simple white shirt?

'What are you doing here?' she demanded, briefly registering Xenon's startled look and the fact that her belligerent demand was not a normal employee-to-boss query.

'You wouldn't take my calls.'

'Are you surprised?'

'With you? Constantly.'

'The reason I didn't take your calls was the same reason why people usually refuse to take calls—because I didn't want to speak to you. And that much hasn't changed. So I'm going.'

'You're not going anywhere until you've heard me out. Xenon, I wonder if you'd mind leaving us?' questioned Zak, his eyes not leaving her face, registering her pallor and the dark shadows around her eyes.

'Xenon, please stay!' Emma chimed in urgently.

'No way! I am *out* of here!' said Xenon, and she

watched with a mixture of disbelief and despair as the big man scrambled to his feet and beat a hasty retreat, still shaking his head. 'She wouldn't take his calls,' he was repeating to himself, in an incredulous voice.

The sound of the slamming door echoed around the room and Emma stood facing her erstwhile lover, her heart beating so fast that she longed to clutch at the desk for support, but didn't dare for fear that it would come over as a sign of weakness. And she wasn't weak, she reminded herself. She was *strong*.

'I've just handed my notice in,' she said, trying not to react to his towering presence and that earthy scent of sandalwood, which made her want to press her nose to his chest and inhale it. *Because she wasn't going to fall for his charismatic presence and sexy Greek charm.* She gave him a defiant stare. 'And there's no point trying to talk me out of it.'

He nodded as he registered the determination which seemed to radiate off her, despite the rather frightening pallor of her cheeks. 'I realise that.'

His agreement took her by surprise. 'You do?'

'I've realised a lot of things, Emma—' His breath felt like sandpaper rasping over his dry throat. 'The main one being that I've really missed you.'

Don't let him sway you with soft words he doesn't really mean. 'You haven't had a chance to miss me,' she scoffed. 'I've barely been gone three days.'

'And what if I told you that they'd been the longest three days of my life?'

'I'd say that maybe you should get yourself a new scriptwriter because that line's as old as hell.'

For a moment he wanted to laugh, until he saw the furious look on her face and realised that she meant it. His voice became softer. 'And what if I told you that I'd been a fool?'

'Then I'd be inclined to agree with you.'

'A total fool,' he said quietly, 'who took the best thing he'd ever had and then threw it away.'

'You live and learn.' She shrugged. 'Maybe you'll know better next time.'

Zak's eyes narrowed as he came up against the solid wall of her resistance. 'But there isn't going to be a next time. Don't you realise what I'm saying to you? That it's you I want, Emma. *You*.'

'And I'm supposed to run around the office, whooping for joy at your sudden change of heart? What's brought this on, Zak—couldn't you find anyone at the party who was easy enough to strip for you?'

'That's not fair!'

"Isn't it? I think it is.'

Frustratedly, he clenched his fists by his sides, wanting to pull her into his arms and kiss away that horrible frozen look on her face—but for the first time in his life, he didn't dare. 'I've missed you,' he said gently. 'And I continue to miss you.'

'No!' Her word rang out, clear as a bell, and she hardened her heart to his narrow-eyed look of surprise. 'These are all just *words*! You only *think* you want me because I had the temerity to walk away from you and no one's ever done that before. It's the thing which drives you, Zak—the need to acquire things which seem out of reach. It's why you were able to start all over again when your family lost all their fortune. It's why you've made such a success of your hotel business. But you're forgetting one thing—that I am not a *hotel*!'

In normal circumstances, he might have made a joke about such a ludicrous statement, but Zak could see from the fierce look on her face that a joke would go down like a lead balloon. And it was dawning on him that she meant it. Every word. That this was not a situation he'd ever faced before and, for the first time in his life, he realised that he was in danger of losing her. That was, if he hadn't already lost her.

He felt a splinter of ice nudging at his heart—because wasn't this what he had always feared? This strange feeling of being out of control—of his happiness being dependent on another person? Was this how his mother had felt, when she'd begged his father not to leave her? How he'd hated to see her wounded vulnerability—and now he wondered if he would be laying himself open to such pain and vulnerability if he dared to let himself get close to Emma.

He could play it safe. He could walk away from her now and after a while he would forget her—his ego and his body restored by the ministrations of one of the many beautiful women who could be his for the taking.

Except he wasn't sure that he *could* forget her. Hadn't he been fighting the way he felt about her since the moment she'd walked into his office with her faded jeans and messy hair? And hadn't that fight been almost unendurable when he'd thought she was involved with his brother?

He had treated her badly; he knew that. He'd said

some terrible things to her—things which couldn't just be brushed over and forgotten about. But he had to take the risk of reaching out to her. Of laying himself open by opening up his heart.

Zak didn't do apologies well—he rarely considered that he had anything to apologise *for*. But now he recognised that he needed to embrace a little humility—that such a thing was necessary for the sustenance of the human spirit—regardless of whether Emma would give him another chance.

'And what if I told you I was sorry?' he questioned quietly. 'Deeply and desperately sorry. What then, Emma? Would that work?'

She looked at him, her heart beating very fast. 'Work for what, precisely? Me continuing to design for your hotel group?'

'Damn my hotel group!' he exploded. 'I'm talking about you—and me. About you being my woman!'

His unsophisticated declaration rang through the air and Emma thought how she would have responded if he'd made it a few days ago. How she would have flung herself in his arms and shouted yes, yes, *yes*! Wasn't it strange how, in life, timing was everything?

She cared for Zak—cared for him deeply enough to call it love—and something told her he cared for her, too. Because deep down she wasn't foolish enough to think that he'd followed her back to England just because his pride had been hurt. But she realised that they both had to be sure about their feelings. Surer than just a few passionate words tossed out in the wake of a blazing row. There was too much to lose—for both of them.

He'd been hurt, and she couldn't bear to see him hurt again. And she was thinking about herself, too. Why would she lay herself open to unnecessary heartache if such a thing could be avoided?

'I'm sorry, Zak.' She looked at him, her gaze very steady. 'You'll have to try harder than that.'

CHAPTER THIRTEEN

'How hard?' questioned Zak.

Emma set her mouth into a firm line as the bus juddered its way up the busy London street, not quite believing that they were sitting side by side like this, their thighs almost touching. And that she was finding her determination to keep him at arm's length, the biggest temptation of her life. But if she'd been that determined, then she wouldn't have agreed to let him accompany her home after their spat in Xenon's office, would she? 'I haven't decided.'

'Now you sound like a dominatrix,' he said softly.

'In your dreams.'

He let that one go—mainly because he was aware that she was giving him a second chance and he didn't want to blow it. They were sitting at the top of a red double-decker bus which was taking them to Emma's flat, having left the Granchester. Her idea. But there had been a lot of her ideas floating around this morning—and Zak realised that, for once, he was letting someone else call the shots.

'You know, I've never been on a London bus before,' he observed.

'Always chauffeur-driven cars, I suppose?'

'Pretty much.'

'Then the experience will be good for you.'

He smiled as they passed the silver-encrusted gates of Hyde Park. He still hadn't kissed her. He hadn't even *touched* her. But then, she still hadn't forgiven him and there remained the very bleak possibility that she might not.

'So why are you taking me to your apartment?' he questioned.

'Because it suddenly occurred to me that you don't even know where I live. You've never even seen my home. We've been living in some kind of bubble, Zak— with hardly any contact with the outside world.'

And Zak realised with an ache that he envied her that. Because he didn't really have anywhere he thought of as home. There were the luxurious suites he kept in all his hotels, which he'd customised with the odd painting or piece of furniture. And there was the island he owned in the Myrtoan Sea, with the beautiful house not far from the beach—but when was the last time he'd been there? At least Emma had somewhere that she thought of as completely hers.

'I suppose there'll be loads of your ex-husband's paraphernalia there?' he growled.

'Such as?'

He shrugged, trying to rid himself of this dark feeling of jealousy that she'd actually been married to someone else. Because he'd never done jealousy before—at least, not until he'd thought that his brother had landed himself the most knockout blonde in the world and that he would have to spend a lifetime suppressing the way he felt about her. 'Platinum discs. Music awards. That kind of thing.'

'It's not a shrine, Zak,' she said quietly. 'Nearly all Louis's stuff had to be sold off to pay for his mother's medical care and the debts from his gambling and drug habit.'

Her simple words made all his jealousy melt away— and in its place rushed a great wave of protectiveness, so that suddenly he wanted to catch hold of her and tell her that *he* would protect her. That he would keep all the harsh, dark realities of life away from her door— until he realised that to do that would be to insult her. Because hadn't she done a pretty good job of overcoming those hardships—all on her own?

The bus began to slow and Emma stood up. 'We're here,' she said, inadvertently brushing against him so that just for one brief moment he caught a drift of roses and vanilla—a scent which transported him back to the lazy bliss he had known in her arms. Gritting his teeth behind a grim smile, he followed her down the narrow stairway of the bus until they were standing on a shiny, rain-soaked pavement.

'Where are we?'

Emma laughed. 'It's Hammersmith—not Mars! But I guess you've never been here?'

'You're saying that my horizons are limited?'

'I think we've both been guilty of having limited horizons,' she told him truthfully as she led the way up the stairs at the front of the large and rather ugly red-brick house. People were often surprised when they first saw where she lived—as if they expected the ex-wife of a famous rock-star to be living in some palatial mansion with golden taps and leopard-skin sofas.

But Emma had walked away from her marriage with only the most humble of settlements and she was proud of the home she'd created. The rooms were high-ceilinged and spacious and there were many of the original features still in place. She'd painted the walls a flat, putty-coloured shade, which provided just the right neutral backdrop for each carefully chosen piece of furniture.

Zak looked around, aware of a sense of peace settling over him. 'It's beautiful,' he said softly.

She smiled, some of the tension leaving her body—aware that his praise meant a lot to her, whether she wanted it to or not. 'Seriously?'

'Seriously. But your taste has never been in any question, Emma—that's one of the things which makes you so good at your job.'

She looked at him. 'And what are the other things?'

He shrugged. 'A fearlessness which makes you stand up to your brutish boss?'

'You're not brutish,' she protested as the last of her anger began to trickle away.

'Oh, yes, I am,' he answered. 'Or maybe I can amend that to the past tense. *Was* brutish—but not any more. You see—you take the brutishness right out of me, Emma Geary.'

His grey eyes blazed and Emma felt a fierce wrench of longing. It would have been so easy to cross the room and to fall into his arms. To wrap her arms around his neck and tangle her fingers in his thick black hair, the way she'd done so many times before. But something told her that would be the wrong thing to do. That desire had often clouded all the getting-to-know-you bits. And that if they couldn't do this other stuff—the everyday and often mundane stuff—then they didn't have a hope in hell.

'Coffee?' she questioned as they walked into the sitting room.

Coffee was the last thing he wanted. All he wanted was to kiss her. To somehow make that tight little look disappear from her face. To lose himself in her sweet embrace. And then tumble her down onto that squashy-looking velvet sofa in the corner and make love to her. But Zak recognised that he was going to have to continue to let Emma call the shots, no matter how much his masterful instincts fought against it.

He nodded his agreement. 'Perfect.'

She turned and left the room, where he could hear the sounds of china being clanked around and cupboard doors being opened and closed. Ordinarily, he might have run his eyes over the books which were lined up on the shelves, but he was finding it hard to concentrate on anything. Even the street scene outside was nothing but a muted blur to his preoccupied gaze.

Minutes later, Emma returned with a tray on which stood a cafetiere of strong dark coffee and she poured them each a cup, which neither of them touched.

She was looking at him and once again he was struck by the dark blue shadowing of her eyes—stark against her pale skin. 'Did you know that Nat's in love?' he questioned, watching her reaction very carefully.

'He texted me something on those lines.' She narrowed her eyes. 'And do you approve? Or will you be going out of your way to separate them?'

'Ouch,' he said wryly, meeting the candid sweep of her gaze and realising that she still hadn't forgiven him. 'I guess I deserve that.'

'Yes, you do.'

'Actually, I haven't met her and I know very little about her—other than that she's Greek and he's there with her at the moment.'

'Then maybe you do approve?' she ventured.

'It's none of my business who he marries.' He met her gaze. Held it with the intensity of his own. And prayed that she could read the truth in his next words. 'I'm not doing the control thing with other people any more. I was a fool to ever think I could.'

The room was very quiet and Emma's heart turned over as she stared into the brooding contemplation of his grey eyes. 'Not a fool, Zak,' she said softly. 'Never that. You only wanted to protect him, the way you'd been protecting him all your life. But Nat's an adult now and he has to do it all on his own. You have to let him go.'

A terrible pain tore through his heart as he thought of another scenario—one which was just as likely. 'And what about you, Emma?' he questioned unsteadily. 'Am I going to have to let you go, as well? Has my controlling nature and my instinct to push you away succeeded? Am I too late?'

She shook her head, her throat too thick with emotion to speak—and maybe he realised that because he crossed the room to stand before her, but didn't pull her into his arms with his usual wild passion. Instead, he framed her face with his hands—more tenderly than he'd ever touched her before.

'Am I?' he repeated, because she needed to be sure about this. And he needed to show her that he was capable of humility, as well as love. 'Am I too late?'

'No, Zak,' she whispered. 'You're just in time—and I'll stay with you for ever. That's if you want me to.'

'And what else would I want?' he questioned simply. 'When I love you so much?'

'Oh, Zak.'

He swallowed down the stupid lump which had risen in his throat. 'Is that the only response I get to the declaration of my life?'

Biting back her tears, she nodded, still too overcome to speak. And besides, she didn't want to tell him that she loved him merely as a sort of tit-for-tat thing, because surely he knew by now that she loved him with all her heart? But perhaps she ought to tell him anyway…

'Zak,' she whispered.

'Shh.' His smile was soft but his lips were hard as they claimed hers in a kiss.

Zak realised that the most important moments in his life had all been about Emma—but none was quite as profound as that first kiss they shared after he'd told her that he loved her.

EPILOGUE

THEY were married in the wedding room at the Pembroke, because it seemed crazy not to—although to Emma the idea felt a little spooky at first.

'Why spooky?' Zak had questioned curiously, his fingers stroking idly through her long hair.

'Oh, because it's almost as if, in my subconscious, I was designing it for me.' She glanced over at the statue of the Greek goddess, Aphrodite—which the trade press had made so much fuss about—and she smiled. Maybe she had.

In fact, she was exactly the four-hundredth bride to marry there—because she'd wanted to enjoy the two of them just being together for a while, and because the Pembroke was currently *the* place for couples to exchange their vows. The waiting list was over a year long and Zak's competitors were eyeing him with ill-concealed envy. There had been a big spread in one of the financial magazines all about the Greek tycoon with the 'Midas touch.' But he told anyone who'd listen that it was his fiancée's touch which turned the world to gold. His *'chrisi mou.'* His golden one.

It was a big, noisy Greek wedding and it seemed to symbolise the warmth of a family life which neither of them had ever had. Nat was there with Chara, his fiancée. A very different Nat from the one Emma had left behind in London. When he'd discovered that she and Zak were in love, he had squared up to his big brother—threatening to pulverise him if he ever harmed one hair of Emma's golden head, or made her cry.

And Zak had let him. He had stood there and taken it. It had been sweet and rather *primitive* to watch, thought Emma. Like two mighty beasts of the jungle each marking out their own territory.

Leda came too, with Scott, her face wreathed with smiles—although she did murmur, 'I can't believe it!' as she leaned forward to give Emma a congratulatory kiss.

Zak and Emma honeymooned on his beautiful island in the Myrtoan Sea, just off the southernmost end of the Peloponnese. It was the island which the Constantinides family had once owned—and then lost—until Zak had bought it back again. He gifted it to Emma on the morning of their wedding and she looked at him with shining eyes and some bemusement.

'But why? Why are you giving me this?'

'Because I want you to own a part of my country,' he replied simply. 'And therefore, a part of me.'

What woman wouldn't thrill to such a declaration? thought Emma delightedly as she wound her arms around his neck.

It was later that same year, during Nat's own wedding to Chara, that Emma discovered she was pregnant—but not wanting to detract from the newly-weds' excitement, she waited until they were back in England before she told Zak the news. In fact, she waited until she'd done two tests and the doctor had told her that she was in the best of health. And still she felt as if she had to keep pinching herself—as if she couldn't quite believe how lucky she was.

The Garden room at the Granchester had just been awarded another Michelin star and Zak and Emma were going there for a celebratory lunch being hosted by Xenon—to the place where their love affair had started.

Outside the main entrance, she paused for a moment and laid her fingers on his arm.

'Zak?'

He turned to look down at her, his eyes tender—wondering if this much contentment could possibly be good for a man. 'Mmm?'

'I've got something to tell you.'

'Sounds big.'

'It is big.' She paused. 'Or rather, I will be—in a few months' time.'

His eyes widened. 'Emma?'

'Zak?'

'You're having a baby?'

'I am.' She grinned. 'Actually, I'm having *your* baby.'

With a small moan of joy, he gathered her in his arms, looking down at her for one intense and loving moment. 'Thank you,' he said softly, in a voice which wasn't quite steady, before he began to kiss her.

She clung to him as if it were the first time they'd ever kissed—but with Zak, every kiss felt a bit like that—and Emma lost herself in the passion of the moment. She forgot that they were on a busy pavement and that the rest of the guests would be waiting. She forgot everything except the feeling of being in his arms and the sheer joy of their mutual love—until suddenly she became aware that cars were tooting at them. The cacophony of sound was difficult to ignore and, reluctantly, they drew apart as a lorry pulled up alongside them—and a boy of about sixteen leaned out of the passenger window.

'Oi!' he yelled. 'Why don't you two get a room?'

Zak smiled as he looked up at the glittering frontage of the Granchester hotel before turning back to his wife. 'Somehow,' he murmured, 'I don't think that's going to be a problem.'

* * * * *

COMING NEXT MONTH from Harlequin Presents®
AVAILABLE AUGUST 21, 2012

#3083 CONTRACT WITH CONSEQUENCES
Miranda Lee
Scarlet wants a baby, but ruthless John Mitchell's help comes with a devilish price—that they do it the old-fashioned way!

#3084 DEFYING THE PRINCE
The Santina Crown
Sarah Morgan
Scandalized singer Izzy Jackson is whisked away from the baying press by Prince Matteo...straight from the limelight into the fire....

#3085 TO LOVE, HONOR AND BETRAY
Jennie Lucas
Callie never imagined that on her wedding day she would be kidnapped by her boss, Eduardo Cruz—the father of her unborn baby.

#3086 ENEMIES AT THE ALTAR
The Outrageous Sisters
Melanie Milburne
Sienna Baker is the last woman Andreas Ferrante would ever marry. But now she's the key to his inheritance!

#3087 DUTY AND THE BEAST
Desert Brothers
Trish Morey
Princess Aisha is rescued from the clutches of a lascivious prince by barbarian Zoltan. Now he must marry Aisha to ensure he's crowned king.

#3088 A TAINTED BEAUTY
What His Money Can't Buy
Sharon Kendrick
Ciro D'Angelo discovers his "perfect wife" isn't as pure as he'd thought! Yet once you're a D'Angelo wife—there's no escape....

COMING NEXT MONTH from Harlequin Presents® EXTRA
AVAILABLE SEPTEMBER 4, 2012

#213 GIANNI'S PRIDE
Protecting His Legacy
Kim Lawrence
Can Gianni conquer his pride and admit that he might
have met his match in utterly gorgeous Miranda?

#214 THE SECRET SINCLAIR
Protecting His Legacy
Cathy Williams
One spectacular night under Raoul's skilful touch leads
to consequences Sarah could never have imagined: she's
pregnant with the Sinclair heir!

#215 WHAT HAPPENS IN VEGAS...
Inconveniently Wed!
Kimberly Lang
Evie's scandalous baby bombshell will provide
tantalising gossip-column fodder, unless she marries the
dangerously attractive billionaire Nick Rocco...father of
her baby!

#216 MARRYING THE ENEMY
Inconveniently Wed!
Nicola Marsh
Ruby finds herself propositioning tycoon Jax Maroney
in order to save her family's company—but it's only a
marriage on paper...isn't it?

REQUEST YOUR
FREE BOOKS!

2 FREE NOVELS PLUS
2 FREE GIFTS!

PASSION GUARANTEED SEDUCTION

YES! Please send me 2 FREE Harlequin Presents® novels and my 2 FREE gifts (gifts are worth about $10). After receiving them, if I don't wish to receive any more books, I can return the shipping statement marked "cancel." If I don't cancel, I will receive 6 brand-new novels every month and be billed just $4.30 per book in the U.S. or $4.99 per book in Canada. That's a saving of at least 14% off the cover price! It's quite a bargain! Shipping and handling is just 50¢ per book in the U.S. and 75¢ per book in Canada.* I understand that accepting the 2 free books and gifts places me under no obligation to buy anything. I can always return a shipment and cancel at any time. Even if I never buy another book, the two free books and gifts are mine to keep forever.
106/306 HDN FERQ

Name	(PLEASE PRINT)

Address	Apt. #

City	State/Prov.	Zip/Postal Code

Signature (if under 18, a parent or guardian must sign)

Mail to the **Reader Service:**
IN U.S.A.: P.O. Box 1867, Buffalo, NY 14240-1867
IN CANADA: P.O. Box 609, Fort Erie, Ontario L2A 5X3

Not valid for current subscribers to Harlequin Presents books.

**Are you a current subscriber to Harlequin Presents books
and want to receive the larger-print edition?
Call 1-800-873-8635 or visit www.ReaderService.com.**

* Terms and prices subject to change without notice. Prices do not include applicable taxes. Sales tax applicable in N.Y. Canadian residents will be charged applicable taxes. Offer not valid in Quebec. This offer is limited to one order per household. All orders subject to credit approval. Credit or debit balances in a customer's account(s) may be offset by any other outstanding balance owed by or to the customer. Please allow 4 to 6 weeks for delivery. Offer available while quantities last.

Your Privacy—The Reader Service is committed to protecting your privacy. Our Privacy Policy is available online at www.ReaderService.com or upon request from the Reader Service.

We make a portion of our mailing list available to reputable third parties that offer products we believe may interest you. If you prefer that we not exchange your name with third parties, or if you wish to clarify or modify your communication preferences, please visit us at www.ReaderService.com/consumerschoice or write to us at Reader Service Preference Service, P.O. Box 9062, Buffalo, NY 14269. Include your complete name and address.

Harlequin® Romance author **Barbara Wallace** *brings you
a romantic new tale of finding love unexpectedly in*
MR. RIGHT, NEXT DOOR!

Enjoy this sneak-peek excerpt.

"It's too beautiful a day to spend stuck inside. Come with me."

"I can't. I have to work."

"Yes, you can," Grant replied, closing the last couple of steps between them and tucking a finger underneath her chin. "You know you want to."

"So, you're a mind reader now?" The response might have worked better if her jaw weren't quivering from his touch.

"Not a mind reader," he replied. "Eye reader. And yours are saying an awful lot."

His touch was making her insides quiver. She wanted desperately to look away and refuse to make eye contact with him, but pride wouldn't let her. Instead, she forced herself to keep her features as bland as possible so he wouldn't see that a part of her—the very female part—did want to go with him. It also wanted to feel more of his touch, and the common sense part of her was having a hard time forming an opposing argument.

"If so, then no doubt you know they're saying 'remove your hand.'"

He chuckled. Soft and low. *A bedroom laugh.* "Did you know they flash when you're being stubborn?"

Rather than argue, Sophie swallowed her pride and looked to his feet.

"You so don't want me to move my hand, either."

"You're incorrigible. You know that, right?"

"Thank you."

"I still want you to move your hand."

"If you insist…." Suddenly his hands were cupping her cheeks, drawing her parted lips under his. Sophie's gasp was lost in her throat. As she expected, he tasted of peppermint and coffee and…and….

And, oh wow, could he kiss!

It ended and her eyelids fluttered open. Grant's face hovered a breath from hers. Gently, he traced the slope of her nose and smiled.

"Your eyes told me you wanted that, too."

If she had an ounce of working brain matter, Sophie would have turned and stormed out of his apartment then and there. Problem was one, she was trembling and, two, the fact she kissed him back probably wiped out any outrage she'd be trying to convey.

So she did the next best thing. She folded her arms across her chest and presented him with a somewhat flushed but indignant expression. "Do not do that again."

Will Grant convince Sophie to let her guard down long enough to see if he's her MR. RIGHT, NEXT DOOR? Find out in September 2012, from Harlequin® Romance!